EARTH'S LAST WAR

PART FOUR OF THE CONTINGENCY WAR SERIES

G J OGDEN

Published by Ogden Media Ltd
ISBN-13: 978-1-9160426-6-7

Cover design by germancreative
Editing by S L Ogden

www.ogdenmedia.net

THE CONTINGENCY WAR SERIES

No-one comes in peace. Every being in the galaxy wants something, and is willing to take it by force...

READ THE OTHER BOOKS IN THE SERIES:

- The Contingency
- The Waystation Gambit
- Rise of Nimrod Fleet
- Earth's Last War

ACKNOWLEDGEMENTS

Thanks to Sarah for her work assessing and editing this novel, and to those who subscribed to my newsletters and provided such valuable feedback.

And thanks, as always, to anyone who is reading this. It means a lot. If you enjoyed it, please help by leaving a review on Amazon and Goodreads to let other potential readers know what you think!

If you'd like updates on future novels by G J Ogden, please consider subscribing to the mailing list. Your details will be used to notify subscribers about upcoming books from this author, in addition to a hand-selected mix of book offers and giveaways from similar SFF authors.

http://subscribe.ogdenmedia.net

ONE

Captain Taylor Ray shuffled to the edge of the command chair and leaned forward while the Contingency One continued to press its pursuit of the enemy ship, as if this would give their scorpion-like Corvette a burst of extra speed. Casey Valera's silver simulant eyes were immersed inside the pilot's viewport as she wrestled with the controls, managing to coax the aging cruiser into performing maneuvers that seemed to defy the laws of physics.

"Get ready, Blakey, one enemy cruiser, coming right up!" called out Casey. She had anticipated the enemy ship's desperate and obvious attempts to evade her and was setting it up perfectly for a volley from the ship's forward cannons.

Blake glanced across and smiled at Casey, even

though she couldn't see him with her eyes inside the viewport, "Just line 'em up and I'll light 'em up..."

A burst from the enemy cruiser's aft turret snaked harmlessly past the Contingency One, before it made another last-ditch attempt to shake Taylor's smaller, nimbler craft. But Casey knew exactly where it was going to end up.

"All yours..." Casey called out, pulling her eyes out of the viewport while simultaneously kicking her shamrock-green sneakers up onto the console and staring expectantly at the viewport.

Blake took over navigational control of the ship in those final seconds, letting loose with both the forward cannons and turrets, landing direct hits with every shot. "Boom!" he shouted, punching the air like Rocky Balboa after beating Ivan Drago, "Another one bites the dust! That's ten today – a new personal best."

"Great work, everyone," said Taylor standing up. "End battle drill and stand down from simulated weapons. Casey, bring us to a full stop."

"Aye, aye, Captain Taylor Ray," said Casey, scooting her feet off the console, before spinning the ship around and pulsing the main engines to counteract their velocity.

"They're gettin' a lot better," said Blake, leaning back casually in his seat, "That last one even managed to land a couple hits on us."

"I bet that's the most times you've been hit on in your life," said Casey, tilting her head in his direction and shooting him a mischievous smile.

"It's not his fault!" laughed Taylor. "I mean, technically, he's less than a month old, you can't expect him to have much game."

Blake scowled, "Hey, leave off the new guy, will ya?"

An incoming message alert bleeped on the mission ops console and James Sonner checked it. He'd had precious little to do for the last five simulated battle drills they'd run, on account of the rookie Nimrod crews failing valiantly to deliver any significant simulated damage to the Contingency One. "It's Commander Sonner, Captain," said James, "she's asking for an update."

Taylor huffed out a laugh, "Colonel Collins is asking, more like," he grumbled, and the others nodded knowingly. "Order Nimrods Charlie Two, Four and Five back to base and get the next two on the starting line, then put Commander Sonner through."

"Aye, Captain," said James, thankful of having something to do. A few moments later the image of Commander Sarah Sonner appeared on the viewport, with the silver-haired and mustachioed Colonel Chester Collins at her side.

"How's it going up there, Captain?" asked Sonner, cheerfully, "Have any of them actually managed to shoot anywhere near you yet?"

Taylor was about to answer, but Collins cut in, and unlike Sonner there was a distinct lack of cheer in his voice, "This is hardly a joking matter, Commander," he snapped, and unseen to him Sonner rolled her eyes. Taylor had to force his jaw shut to make sure he didn't grin and give her away. "We're about to send this fleet into battle, and the Hedalt Armada won't be using simulated weapons."

"Colonel, half of these crews are greener than Casey's sneakers," Taylor replied, but was then distracted as Collins appeared to be trying to check on Casey's footwear through the viewport. Casey quickly tucked her feet underneath the pilot's console and smiled back innocently. "Considering how recently we assembled these crews, they're doing far better than I'd expect."

"Then your expectations are too low!" Collins hit back. "This is not a game, there are real lives at stake."

The use of the phrase, 'real lives' hadn't been lost on Taylor; the Colonel had made no attempt to hide his misgivings about himself, Casey and Blake. Taylor did have some sympathy for his predicament, though. That the Colonel struggled to trust three simulants that were formerly under the control of the Hedalt Empire wasn't in itself all that surprising. Simulants had been instrumental in Earth Fleet losing the war, so Taylor had never expected to be welcomed into the fold with open arms. And, in truth, Collins hadn't be the only one to eye them with a palpable degree of suspicion and mistrust; many of the other Earth Fleet officers and crew were also wary of them. But that Taylor's actions and the actions of his crew, and even Collins' own direct interactions with him, had not further informed his views was surprising. It demonstrated how intransigent – or, as Sonner had put it, 'arrogant, pig-headed and blinkered' – their new Commander was. Taylor may have been less harsh in his own description, but there was no doubt that Colonel Collins was inflexible and incapable of adapting to the new reality he'd been confronted with after waking from hibernation.

Part of that new reality was that not all simulants were the enemy, but in general the situation on the ground was radically removed from what anyone at Earth Fleet had anticipated at the time the Contingency was put into action. Commander Sarah Sonner was the only one to survive the failure of the hibernation systems on the main Contingency base, and the cobbled-together remains of humanity, recovered from the asteroid repair base and the reserve base, had found themselves three centuries further into the future than planned. These inexperienced crews and the ninety-nine Nimrod-class cruisers were hopelessly outmatched and outgunned by the sophisticated and far larger Hedalt ships that had been deployed since. But Collins had been adamant that they should stick to the original Contingency battle plans; plans that Sonner and Taylor agreed were now completely outdated and irrelevant. And this made Colonel Collins just as dangerous as an armada of Hedalt War Frigates.

"We're running live and simulated battle scenarios around the clock, Colonel," Taylor replied, a hint of exasperation creeping into his voice. "Unless you know of another hidden base with a few hundred battle-hardened captains in stasis inside, we're doing all we can."

"It's not enough," Collins retorted, "you must train harder."

Sonner then added her voice in support of Taylor, "Look, Colonel, the only way these crews will get significantly better is with time – time that was factored in to the original Contingency timeline. Delay the attack. Give us the time we need to get these crews up to speed, and come up with a new battle plan."

"We don't have time to delay, Commander," barked Collins, "Surprise is our best weapon, and the longer we wait, the more we risk losing this vital element."

It was a tired argument that Sonner knew she wouldn't win, but Collins' stubborn refusal to see reason irked her enough that she was still unable to let it go. She was about to argue back when an alert sounded on the bridge.

James was on it like a flash, "Jump signature detected..." he said, anxiously waiting for the initial analysis to flash up on the screen. Then he looked at Taylor, eyes wide. "Captain, a Hedalt ship has just entered the system!"

TWO

James Sonner's unexpected report acted like a whetstone, sharpening the senses of everyone on the bridge. Taylor's simulant frame spared him from the fight-or-flight flutters that had suddenly crippled James, allowing him to remain focused. He knew exactly what to do – he just didn't know for sure if it would work.

"Commander, an enemy ship just jumped in," Taylor announced to the startled faces of Sonner and Collins on the viewport. "Deactivate the transmitter on the moon's surface. Do it right now!" He then turned back to James, "Shut down the transmission, do it fast!"

Despite the sudden rush of dizziness and nausea that James experienced, he managed to cut the link to the transmitter on the moon's surface, removing the shocked faces of Collins and Sonner from the viewport. Taylor's simulant eyes detected the young officer's trembling hands and flushed face, but now more than ever he needed him to have a clear head; their survival depended on it. Taylor rushed to James' side and dropped a hand on his shoulder, which acted like an anchor that steadied him both physically and emotionally. Then, calmly, as if the situation was nothing more serious than a drill, he added, "Cut main power and run silent, James. Do it as quick as you can. And reduce life support to minimum."

"Aye, Captain," James replied, initiating the emergency shutdown process to rig the ship for silent running. He was grateful for the weight of Taylor's hand on his shoulder, keeping him grounded and counteracting the lightness in his head that threatened to float him off the chair.

The omnipresent hum of energy conduits started to diminish and Taylor heard the fans that circulated air and heat around the ship spin down. He patted James' shoulder, "Sorry, Technical Specialist, but it might get a little chilly in here for a time."

"Aye, Captain, I'll manage," James answered, keeping a brave face, though his voice wobbled ever so slightly.

"Order the four Nimrod captains to run silent too, alpha priority," Taylor continued. "Use radio waves and encode as text only, full encryption. Keep the transmission power to the absolute minimum you can get away with. With any luck, whatever that ship is out there, they won't be listening for something as archaic as VHF radio."

The lights on the bridge shut off so that the only illumination was from photo-luminescent emergency lighting strips and the soft glow of the critical computer consoles that remained active.

"Engines down, reactor to minimal output, Captain," said Casey. "We're as quiet as any spaceship could be, without becoming an icicle."

"Message received by the Nimrods," James added. "Local heat and EM signatures are dropping off significantly, so I think they heard us. But there's no way that we can completely hide the fact we're out here."

"I know, James," Taylor replied, again ensuring his tone was as warm and reassuring as it could be, given the circumstances. But he wasn't about to feed him false hope either. "We've done our jobs well, so all we can do now is hope that the Hedalt's attention is focused elsewhere."

The phrase 'silent running' was something of a misnomer when it came to starships, since there was no way to completely mask their signature. But it was also a big star system and the Hedalt vessel would need some time to calibrate its scanners after jumping in. So long as they had acted quickly enough, there was a good chance of remaining undetected, providing the enemy ship wasn't specifically looking for them.

An eerie silence crept over the bridge, which only served to highlight just how much noise the hundreds of different ship's systems actually made. Without them, Taylor could hear the creak of metal and even the sound of James Sonner's breathing, rapid and shallow. To distract himself, Taylor studied the data displayed on the single console screen that had remained functioning on the mission ops station. It was showing all the passive sensor data they had collected before shutting down, including the limited information that James had managed to compile about their intruder. He was perfectly capable of interpreting the information himself, but he also knew that giving Sonner a task would help to keep his mind off their dangerous situation.

"Talk to me, Mr. Sonner, who is our new friend out there?"

James brought up the limited tactical scan data on the console screen. "There's not much to say, Captain, but it's definitely Hedalt," he began, rubbing his hands together; the bridge was already starting to get colder. "It's small, less than half the size of the Contingency One. Assuming it remains on course, its last know trajectory would put it heading towards the far side of the fourth planet in the system, relative to our position."

"What, the same planet this miserable, dusty rock's orbitin'?" said Blake appearing just behind Taylor with Casey alongside. James Sonner nodded and Blake folded his arms, "Damn, that's a little too close for comfort. What's there that it could want? It's just another dead rock, ain't it?"

"Yes, it is..." said Taylor idly, though he was thinking hard. *The far side of the planet?... Of all the planets in the galaxy, why would a Hedalt scout go there?* Then he remembered, and he snapped his fingers, as if it was a eureka moment. "The crashed Nimrod... They're returning to the crash site."

"The crashed what-now?" said Blake, dipping his chin and cocking his head ever so slightly to the side in disapproval. If he'd had eyebrows, they would have been raised all the way up.

"When Commander Sonner and I first left the Contingency base, we crashed a Nimrod on the surface to act as a decoy, should the Hedalt ever come looking for their missing Hunter Corvette," Taylor explained. "We took the transceiver from the Contingency One and put it on the Nimrod, so that it would look like a crashed Hedalt ship to anyone in orbit."

"Smart," said Blake, with genuine appreciation. "So if the Hedalt found it, they'd just think you had some kinda simulant brain-fart that caused you to crash, an' not bother to go snoopin' 'round the rest of the system."

Casey leaned in towards Blake with a disgusted look on her face, and whispered to him, "Brain fart?" but Blake just waved her off.

"That was the idea," said Taylor, suppressing a smile to remain serious, even though it was great to see that Casey and Blake's playful interactions were a feature of bridge life once again. "But we have to assume that their arrival now isn't a co-incidence, not after everything that happened at the Hedalt breaking yard. If they discover the crashed ship is actually a Nimrod then they'll run a fine-toothed comb through this star system until they eventually find us."

"So, what do we do, Cap?" asked Casey.

Taylor stroked the smooth synthetic skin on his chin, weighing up their options, but it soon became apparent to him that they had very few available to them. "For now, we wait for that ship to leave."

"And then?" Blake pressed.

"Then, as much as I hate to agree with Collins, we have to get the fleet underway as soon as possible. We can't risk being discovered while the fleet is still underground; they'd be sitting ducks." There were audible exhalations, from human and simulant alike. "But... that doesn't mean we have to go into battle unprepared."

Casey smiled, "Ooh, I like this rebellious new Captain Taylor Ray!"

"It certainly makes a change!" Blake laughed, slapping Taylor on the shoulder a little harder than he had planned, "I take it you have some genius an' prob'ly slightly dumb plan?"

Taylor didn't relish what he had to do next, especially considering the last time he had entered the Fabric, he nearly didn't make it back out alive. And this time, there would be no Sarah Sonner to pull him out if things went south. But if the fleet was going to jump back to Earth, they needed to know exactly what they were dealing with. He met each of their eyes in turn and then said, "I wouldn't say it's a genius plan, and it's certainly a little dumb, but I do have an idea. And it involves me taking a little space walk."

THREE

Provost Adra had been waiting outside the tribunal hearing room in Warfare Command headquarters for over two hours. Her patience was wearing thin. Ever since she had been ordered to return to the Hedalt home world – the core world they had seized from the Masters and adopted as their own – all she had done was wait.

In order to allow time for the random selection of provosts to assemble, the tribunal had been scheduled a week after High Provost Kagan had first confronted Adra on her frigate. In that time, she had been ordered to remain at Warfare Command headquarters, effectively under arrest. She had heard no further news of the humans, nor had she the ability to monitor for incursions into the CoreNet by the rogue simulant. Kagan had ensured that her access to the CoreNet had been tightly restricted. But there had been advantages to the delay too. The first was that it had afforded Adra time to research the signal anomaly in more detail, in an attempt to determine how to better track and disable it, along with its simulant source. The second was that it had allowed her to heal and regain her strength fully. In fact, she felt stronger than he had done for years; a consequence of the forced reprieve from super luminal travel, which took its toll, mentally and physically, even on one as strong as Provost Adra. Regular exposure to the Fabric had a debilitating effect, like ocean waves gradually lapping away at and eroding a coastline, except instead of destroying rock and earth, it wore away at your soul.

The door to the tribunal room opened and a soldier exited and began marching towards Adra. She recognized her as Kagan's Adjutant, who had accompanied the High Provost when he boarded her War Frigate. At the time Adra had not known why the soldier had greeted her with such silent hostility, but since arriving back on the home world, she had discovered the motive. Her name was Vika and she was Adjutant Lux's sister. Vika was lithe and moved with a confidence and fluidity that few soldiers managed to combine with such natural ease. It suggested not only competence, but ability too. This alone told Adra that she was not to be underestimated, but the fact that she served the High Provost directly was evidence enough that her mental and physical talents exceeded those of an average or even proficient soldier.

A blood feud was the least of Adra's concerns, though it irked her that even if she survived the tribunal, a contest with Vika would likely follow. Adra accepted that Vika was within her rights to issue a challenge over the death of her brother. Lux had died under Adra's command, as a direct result of Adra's unauthorized pursuit of the rogue simulant and Hunter Corvette. She had vastly exceeded her orders and authority – she did not need the tribunal to confirm that – and as a result it was the same as if Adra had murdered Lux in cold blood, without justification. But Adra did not fear this young Adjutant. If Vika was to challenge, it would merely be an added inconvenience; one she would deal with as and when it became necessary. First she had to survive High Provost Kagan's judgment.

Vika came to a halt a couple of meters in front of Adra. The hostility shone through in her eyes, just as it had done on the frigate, but when she spoke she conveyed the proper respect owed to an officer of Adra's coveted rank.

"Provost Adra, the tribunal is ready to hear your testimony," said Vika, maintaining eye contact with Adra. "If you would please follow me, I shall escort you inside." Vika then turned side-on to Adra, bowing slightly while extending a hand in the direction of the hearing room.

Adra said nothing in reply and simply began to cross the long corridor towards the hearing room. She kept her pace deliberately slow so as to prolong the journey. Partly, she wanted to give Vika an opportunity to speak, but also she wanted to convey her respects regarding Lux. This was not motivated by guilt – Adra felt no such emotion – nor was it an attempt to placate Vika. Adra genuinely believed that Lux had merited such a tribute. From his beginnings as the jittery and hesitant adjutant who had frustrated Adra, Lux had gone on to prove his mettle and his worth. In the end his loyalty had been absolute. And there was nothing Adra valued more highly than loyalty.

"You are the sister of Lux, are you not?" asked Adra, keeping her eyes forward as she paced ahead with Vika just behind and to her side.

"I was," came the simple response. Still Vika showed no sign of emotion.

"His death was unfortunate," Adra continued, "as my adjutant, he was loyal and performed his duties to my satisfaction."

Vika did not respond immediately, and the silence was filled only by the clack, clack, clack of their boots striking the polished stone floor of

Warfare Command headquarters.

"It pleases me to know that," said Vika, eventually breaking the impasse just as they reached the door to the tribunal hearing room. She turned to face Adra, as a masked combat simulant opened the door and waited for them to progress inside. But Vika remained, staring into Adra's green eyes, which were fractionally below the level of her own. "The High Provost awaits you inside," added Vika, still with a cold detachment.

Adra was impressed. If she had not spoken then Vika would have remained silent until they reached the tribunal room. By instigating a conversation she had given Vika the opportunity to comment, but Vika had kept a firm lid on any feelings that she may have had towards her. Feelings that had been expressed with clarity in her own piercing blue eyes, if not her voice or actions. Nevertheless, Adra still wanted to learn more about Vika's temperament and so decided to push her a little harder.

"He collapsed only a short time before the High Provost boarded my ship," said Adra, mirroring Vika's impersonal delivery. "Had he been a little stronger, he would have survived long enough for you to be reunited with him." Then she left a deliberate pause for emphasis and added, "before his brain seized completely."

Vika's eye twitched, the hatred glowing inside

it burning hotter, but she did not rise to the bait. "It is interesting how quickly fortunes can change, Provost," she said, and despite her dispassionate tone, the implied threat was clear. "I wish you good fortune in the tribunal, so that we may meet again." Vika again turned side-on to Adra and gestured for her to progress.

Adra again waited, willing Vika to give in to her emotions, but the adjutant would no longer meet her gaze. Still, Adra was satisfied with what she had learned, and stepped past Vika into the tribunal room. As she took up her place in the circle of the accused, Adra compared Vika to her former adjutant. Lux had been simple to read and understand, but Vika was more calculating. You did not get to serve the High Provost without possessing an understanding of the politics of Warfare Command, as well as an ability to manipulate it. She was smart enough to know her place, and smart enough to bite her tongue, but she was not smart enough to hide her motives. Adra had not pushed hard, but Vika had made her intentions clear. Should Adra make it through the tribunal with her life, Vika would then try to take it from her.

FOUR

Adra had in the past served on the tribunal board as one of the three Provost Judges many times before, but this was her first time in her genetically-prolonged life that she had ever experienced the setting from her current position inside the circle of the accused. The hearing was a formality since by this stage the Provost Judges had already made their determinations. This had been based on testimony that Adra had given in the preceding days, and on their own evidence-gathering. As a former judge herself, she was well aware of how the available evidence (and how it was interpreted) was heavily influenced by High Provost Kagan. The tribunal itself was arranged to deliver the verdict and, more often than not, swiftly carry out the sentence.

Adra looked up to see High Provost Kagan sitting in the center of the three Provost Judges, with two other provosts positioned slightly lower and further back. Between them they would decide Adra's fate, and since she did not expect mercy from Kagan, much resided on the opinions of the other two judges. Adra knew them both. Both despised her.

The first was Provost Tor, one of the longest-serving and oldest Provosts, and also a longtime opponent of Adra's Hunter Simulant Program. Tor had strongly argued against the use of non-lobotomized human brains inside the simulant frames, believing it would introduce an unstable element and unnecessary risk. The tribunal would give her the ideal opportunity to gloat and prove herself correct. The other was Vice Provost Duma, whom Adra had leapfrogged to attain the rank of provost, and who had carried a personal grudge against her ever since. Kagan knew just as well as Adra that Duma lacked the physical and mental fortitude to be worthy of the rank, and that he would never attain it on merit. His selection to the board was therefore deeply suspicious, given that there had been other full provosts available. Adra had known the selection of board members in advance and so had done some digging only to discover that Duma was on the very short list of names to be promoted to provost during the next round of ascensions. But there were only ever twelve full provosts serving in the entirety of Warfare Command at any one time, which meant that for another to be ascended to provost, first a serving provost had to step down, or die. The obvious conclusion was that Kagan had cut a deal with Duma. A deal that would ultimately mean Adra's demise.

The lights dimmed inside the tribunal chamber, leaving only a few spotlights focused on the three Provost Judges, and the glowing circle of the accused, inside which Adra stood. In the ambient glow of the floor, Adra could see Adjutant Vika standing to the side. That she had not removed herself meant that she still had a part to play in the proceedings, though what part, Adra could not guess. Given how predictable Adra considered the outcome to be, Vika's presence was intriguing and the only unknown variable.

"Provost Adra, the board has reviewed the evidence," Kagan began. His melodic voice was amplified and seemed to assault her from all directions. "Before I summarize our judgment, do you have anything final to add?"

"No, High Provost Kagan, I do not," replied Adra, her own normally resonant voice sounding feeble and insignificant compared to Kagan's, like the bark of a small dog next to the roar of a lion.

"Very well," said Kagan, "then this is the board's

determination."

Screens turned on beneath the raised black metal podium on which the Provost Judges sat, detailing the litany of charges against Adra. She read them, recognizing each charge as being true. She had withheld information of vital importance to the empire from the Warfare Council; specifically, the nature of the signal anomaly and the existence of surviving homo sapiens from Earth. She had neglected her escort duties and given false justification. She had executed Hedalt citizens without due process. She had exceeded her special extra-judicial authority by denying surrendered racketeers a hearing. Through neglect of her duties and abuse of her position, she had allowed two high-functioning simulants to be captured by the enemy. And as a direct result of these indiscretions, she had been personally responsible for the unnecessary death of a military adjutant. Kagan had graciously noted her inventive defeat of racketeer pirates, but beyond this token gesture, the evidence was scathing.

"Provost Adra, do you have anything to say in response to these charges?" came the booming voice of Kagan.

"No, High Provost," Adra replied without delay. She had seen enough tribunals to know how this one would end. Of all the charges that had been leveled against her, the preventable death of Lux was the most severe. Were it not for this charge, as a highly respected provost with a distinguished and flawless record, she would have been granted a dishonorable dismissal. This would mean incarceration for the rest of her life, or however long she managed to survive in a prison camp filled with racketeers and other criminals. But the preventable sacrifice of Lux was unforgivable. That alone merited execution.

"Let the records show that the board of Provost Judges has rejected your submitted defense of these actions," Kagan continued, "As the architect and chief proponent of the high-functioning Hunter Simulant Program, you had a personal stake in ensuring that their failure remained secret. You have acted in the interest of self-preservation, and not in the interest of the Hedalt Empire." Kagan then stood, shortly followed by Provosts Tor and Duma. "Provost Adra, the punishment for these charges is execution. Do you have anything to add before the sentence is carried out?"

"I have nothing to add, High Provost Kagan," replied Adra, again without delay. She had already accepted her fate and knew that within a matter of minutes she would be dead, shot by a firing squad of five combat simulants. Kagan was about to speak again when from the shadows, Adjutant Vika stepped into the circle of the accused. To break the circle was to make a formal intervention, and considering that Kagan had already issued his verdict, it was clear from his furrowed brow that he had not expected it.

Adra also had not expected it. She peered over at Vika with interest, the soft yellow under-glow from the circle casting shadows across her face, distorting her features and oddly making her appear more like her brother. For a moment, Adra half expected Vika to draw a blade and carry out the execution right there in the tribunal room, but instead she turned away from Adra's confused frown and stared up at High Provost Kagan.

"Apologies for the intervention, High Provost Kagan," Vika began confidently, but respectfully, "but I wish to speak on behalf of the accused."

Adra's typically unflappable composure failed her in that moment, but even more remarkable was that Kagan's expression was more shocked than her own. She stared from Vika to Kagan and back again, trying to understand what was happening. But she simply could not comprehend why Vika of all people would speak on her behalf.

"What is your justification?" Kagan grunted, his normally tuneful voice suddenly turning gruff and coarse.

"My brother, Lux, is unable to speak on behalf of his commander," continued Vika, her voice managing to fill the room even without the aid of amplification. "As his only living kin, I received his personal effects, including a journal of the events for which Provost Adra is accused."

"Yes, we have already reviewed those records," Kagan replied, impatiently. "What of them?"

"His records confirm the deep respect and admiration he felt for his commander, and a belief that her actions were just," Vika went on. "Were he alive, I am sure he would stand at her side."

"But he is not alive, Adjutant Vika," Kagan answered testily, clearly losing patience.

"No, and so I stand here in his stead," Vika continued, "and request the right of atonement."

The two other Provost Judges glanced at each other and shuffled uncomfortably, but Kagan did not flinch, nor did he take his accusing eyes off Vika. It was a look Adra had seen before, reflected back at herself in the mirror in her secured quarters after learning the names of the Provost Judges. It was the look she had worn only moments before Vika had taken to the floor. It was the look of someone who had been forced, grudgingly, to accept defeat.

Adra, on the other hand had emerged the victor, through no action of her own. The right of atonement allowed a death sentence to be commuted, but it was only permissible in extraordinary circumstances. Vika's attestation that Lux would have stood with Adra on the floor of the accused certainly counted as extraordinary.

It did not change the improper circumstances of his death, but it turned Lux from victim to willing partner. That Adra had inspired such devotion and loyalty from a subordinate in a military culture driven by loyalty and unwavering conviction could not be simply hand-waved away, even by High Provost Kagan.

"You have that right, Adjutant Vika," Kagan replied, but the razor-sharp edge to his eyes had dulled and his voice intoned melodically again. Then Kagan quickly glanced at Provosts Tor and Duma, each returning a token nod that signified their acceptance, before he peered down at Adra. "Provost Adra, it seems you are to receive a last-second and highly unexpected reprieve." His eyes flicked across to Vika as he said, 'unexpected'. "You are hereby reduced in rank to Vice Provost, a rank that you will never again exceed. You will continue to serve the empire by escorting and protecting freighters in the outer regions. Your War Frigate shall be seized and replaced with a vessel more suited to your lower rank and status - a Destroyer-class battleship."

Adra felt numb as Kagan's revised judgment was announced. The prospect of living out her days as a Vice Provost, escorting insignificant convoys in a mediocre vessel in the most insignificant regions of space appalled her. And that Kagan had assigned her a Destroyer, a vessel little better than the centuries-old Corvette, was intended to add insult to injury. But the worst element of the new sentence was one that Kagan had not expressed explicitly. As Vice Provost, with no hope of ascension, Adra would never be permitted to pursue her studies of Hedalt ancestry on Earth. Adra maintained her composure and did not allow her anger or shame to reveal itself, but she silently cursed Vika for her intervention. A firing squad would be been the greater mercy. Whether this had been Vika's intent or not was unknown, but she would at least live to find out, even if that meant beating the admission from her.

"I understand, High Provost," said Adra, with a wilted bow.

Vika bowed also and then turned with the intention of leaving the circle of the accused, but Kagan was quick to halt her exit. "Adjutant Vika, I have not finished," Kagan said darkly. Vika stopped, glanced up at Kagan suspiciously and then moved back into the center of the circle, alongside Adra. "Vice Provost Adra will require a new adjutant," Kagan continued, his voice now thick and syrupy smooth. Adra immediately knew what was coming next, even though Vika's bemused expression still betrayed her ignorance. She had not only condemned Adra to a fate worse than death – she had condemned herself, also. "In light of your honorable defense of the accused on behalf of your brother, I can think of no-one better than yourself for this duty."

Vika may have been gifted with physical strength and mental fortitude, but she was young and had yet to master Adra's ice cold ability to hide her feelings. The announcement from Kagan was like a knife to her gut and her reaction was so brutal, so raw, that Adra almost felt it herself. But the youthful adjutant at least had the presence of mind to keep her mouth shut. To question Kagan in any way whatsoever would have meant her own execution. And as a mere adjutant, Vika could not expect anything as merciful as a firing squad.

"This tribunal is now concluded," announced Kagan, before rising and leaving the tribunal room through the judge's exit to the rear. Provosts Tor and Duma followed close behind, leaving only Vika and Adra in the room. The lights remained low, maintaining the sinister shadows on each of their faces.

Adra did not believe Vika's intentions were so Machiavellian as to spare her from the firing squad just so that she could enjoy the humiliation of Adra losing her rank and ship and privileged status. Vika did not know her, and Adra had not allowed Lux to get close enough to truly know what drove her and what she feared the most. Vika's motivation must have been far simpler and purer. She wanted Adra to survive so that she could challenge her and take personal revenge for the death of her brother. That she had spoken for Adra in the tribunal did not matter, that was merely an act of honor in respect of her brother, relaying the testimony she believed he would have given at the tribunal, had he the opportunity. But it did not represent Vika's own opinions, nor would it prevent her from issuing a challenge. In fact, as Vika knew just as well as Adra did, the only thing that would prevent Vika from challenging Adra was a direct line of reporting. Kagan knew this too and unlike his former adjutant, the High Provost always acted with calculated intent. By making Vika the adjutant to Adra, High Provost Kagan had taken from her the only thing she wanted. Blood and revenge.

FIVE

Adra felt no connection to her adopted home world and never had done. The Masters were a cold and clinically-minded race, which showed in the simplistic, yet crudely imposing architecture of the cities that blanketed practically the entire surface of the planet. And as she stood on the grand roof terrace atop the Warfare Command building, itself a stark and unimaginative black obelisk that rose fifteen-hundred feet into the steel-gray sky, dislike turned to resentment. She would never now be able to swap the anemic skyline in front of her for the blue skies she longed to see again on Earth.

In the centuries since the conquest and destruction of human-occupied Earth, Warfare Command, with the help of millions of worker simulants, had transformed the planet beyond recognition. The radiation had been neutralized and the devastation undone. But Earth was never to be a populated world again, at least not one populated by sentient creatures. Where cities had once stood, the Hedalt had returned the land to nature. In essence, Earth had been transformed into a planet-wide sanctuary and monument to the Hedaltus race, like a National Park, but on a global scale. Besides simulants and a small number of Hedalt wardens, only a privileged few were allowed to set foot on the surface. And only those who had distinguished themselves in service to the empire were granted permission to settle there upon completion of their tenures. This was an honor granted only to those in the military service. Those who toiled in scientific, artistic, engineering or other disciplines could never be eligible. Only a provost – one of the twelve on the Warfare Council, including Kagan – could receive such an commendation. It had been the sole reason that Adra had enlisted in Warfare Command from the scientific services. It had been the only reason she had spent over two centuries aboard starships – a location she detested only slightly less than the home world. Earth was a privilege that Adra had earned, through tireless devotion to duty and her exceptional contribution to the Hedalt Empire. She was due her rightful place on Earth. But thanks to Vika's intervention and Kagan's judgment, this future had been stripped from her. Vika would never know the depth of the injury she had dealt, and Adra would never let her see it.

Adra could at least take some satisfaction from knowing that Vika too had lost everything she had worked for. As adjutant to Kagan, Vika already held a status far above her age and rank, and if she had continued to serve the High Provost with distinction, she would have quickly ascended into the echelons of the provosts, leapfrogging others as Adra had once done. But now she had gone from adjutant to the most powerful figure in the Hedalt Empire, to adjutant to a disgraced and demoted former provost, who had only escaped execution because of her actions. For Vika, as it was for Adra, it was a stain that would never wash off. She had saved Adra, yet killed them both.

The rhythmic thump of boots stepping in time echoed off the obsidian walls of the terrace. Adra turned to see High Provost Kagan approaching, flanked by two combat simulants in amber-edged, full-cover armor. Following ignominiously behind them was Adjutant Vika, who had already lost the amber edge to her uniform. Without it, she looked somehow more ordinary, but Adra was not foolish enough to consider her any the less lethal. Kagan stopped a few meters short of Adra and rested his hands on the ice-smooth wall, staring out across the monochrome skyline.

"I never tire of this view," Kagan began, sucking the cool, tasteless air into his lungs. The wind barely moved a strand on his slicked back, dark brown hair, which was always so pristine that it appeared almost metallic. Then he looked at Adra, "Do you know why?"

"I do not, High Provost," Adra replied, distracted by the idea of throwing Kagan off the terrace. She wondered what sort of arrangement of blood and smashed flesh and bone he would create on the surface far below. She would have considered the attempt had it not been for the fact that combat simulants would have shot her dead before Kagan had even hit the ground. *What would be the point of killing Kagan if I do not even live long enough to enjoy it?* she considered. Besides, Kagan had done only what she had expected him to do. She did not blame him for his actions any more than she would blame a scorpion for stinging.

"Because it is the representation of conquest and dominance. It is the very landscape of our victory," Kagan explained, adding inflections that made the words sound like poetry. "First, the Masters fell to our superior strength, and then the homo sapiens followed. Or so we thought."

Adra remained silent. As a provost, she might have been able to comment her belief that the Hunter Simulant Program had been ended prematurely, but her new status offered her very little leeway. Kagan watched her carefully, and when it was clear that Adra was not going to respond he took a pace towards her and then stood with his hands behind his back.

"I stood on Earth, amongst the smashed remains of its cities, and crushed the charred and blacked bones of burned humans beneath my feet. I was convinced that we had wiped them out." Kagan paused and then sighed. Even the breath escaping his lungs sounded like music. "It seems you were right after all, Vice Provost Adra," Kagan continued. These were the last words that Adra had expected to hear, but she hid her surprise expertly. "So perhaps it is right also that you still have a role to play. A role that suits your unique abilities and experience. A role that allows you to make recompense for your offenses against the Hedalt Empire."

"I am ready for duty, High Provost," said Adra, intrigued to learn where Kagan was heading with this curious exchange.

"Then go to the Nexus," said Kagan, "I want you to discover a method of tracing these signal anomalies with speed and precision, directly to the source, and to be able to purge them without drawing the anomaly through the Fabric to your location. This rogue simulant has become a virus and it must be eliminated, before it has a chance to infect the CoreNet. I do not need to explain to you the importance of the simulant network."

"I will set to work at once," Adra replied, once again expertly hiding any physical tells from Kagan that would indicate her surprise or satisfaction at the order. The idle time she had spent on the home world while awaiting the tribunal had already given her ample opportunity to study this problem. And so she already had a solution, in theory. The Nexus would give her the chance to test the theory. But, she had no intention of letting Kagan know this; once he had extracted from Adra everything he needed, she would be of no further use, and Adra would be sent thousands of light years away to patrol the empire's outer reaches. She had no intention of spending the rest of her life in such obscurity.

"Then your new ship awaits you, Vice Provost Adra," Kagan replied, melodiously, "as does your new adjutant." Kagan turned and curled his index finger into a hook, beckoning Vika over. Adra's new adjutant arrived smartly and stood tall, though the tension in her shoulders and neck betrayed her obvious discomfort. "As soon as you discover how to trace and purge these anomalies, you are to inform me without delay," Kagan added, addressing Adra only. He then turned his back on them both without acknowledging or even looking at Vika, and marched away, passing between his two combat simulant escorts, which spun sharply on their heels and pursued with robotic precision.

Adra turned her back on Vika too, knowing that there was a risk of a knife in the back, but also knowing that she had to assert her authority over this new adjutant quickly and – if necessary – brutally. But if she had read Vika correctly, killing Adra in such a dishonorable fashion was not her style, nor would it satisfy her thirst. Vika would want to beat Adra, and would want Adra to know she had been bested before the light left her eyes. But there was another reason Adra had turned, which was so that she could peer up into the cloudless sky at the Nexus, clearly visible orbiting the planet. Although Adra despised the Masters almost as much as she did humans, she could not fail to admire their extraordinary technological achievement in creating it. The Nexus was a space station the size of a planetoid, and it was directly responsible for controlling each and every one of the billions of simulants in operation on the innumerable ships, space stations and planets that comprised the Hedalt Empire. Every super-luminal transceiver in the galaxy fed directly into the Nexus, which acted like a hive mind for the lobotomized simulants. It allowed them to perform the many complex and varied functions that were essential to the smooth functioning of the empire. Everything from farming, to medical skills, to starship piloting were possible only because of the Nexus. Without it there would be no simulants, with the unique exception of the four high-functioning models that Adra had designed. These had been granted independent thought, so that they could operate autonomously, adapting and thinking and using their intelligence to seek out surviving pockets of humanity. Despite its incredible capabilities, the Nexus was no more intelligent than a data pad. It was simply a giant computer, incapable of the sophistication of a fully-formed mind. But its unique connection to the CoreNet and to every super-luminal node in the galaxy also made it the ideal tool to trace and purge the signal anomaly, should it appear again.

"I am ready for duty, Vice Provost Adra," came the voice of Adjutant Vika, after it had become patently obvious that Adra was not going to acknowledge her presence.

Adra was impressed that Vika had managed to expel the sentence with at least some level of sincerity. She kept her back to Vika and continued to stare up at the Nexus. "Go to the ship and get it ready for launch."

"Yes, Vice Provost. What is our destination?" asked Vika.

Adra turned slowly and met Vika's eyes. "Our destination is wherever I tell you to go," she snarled. "You do not ask questions. You obey. Is that understood?"

Vika peered back into Adra's piercing green eyes; the tension between them was explosive and on a hair trigger. It felt like if either had taken a step towards the other, a chain reaction would start that would blow the top right off the black obelisk in which they stood. Vika wanted to kill her, but she also believed herself better than Adra. Stronger. More honorable. More worthy. Now was not the proper moment. But she vowed that the time would come when Adra would lie broken at her feet. She bowed her head by barely half a degree, and said, "It is understood, Vice Provost."

SIX

A War Frigate loomed large in the center of the viewport, plasma cannons trained on Adra's Destroyer-class battleship, while it waited for their security codes to be approved. The vessel dwarfed her own new ship, like an eagle staring down at a starling, but it wasn't just any frigate – it was Adra's former command. She did not know to whom Kagan had assigned it, as the vessel had merely communicated brusquely via text only, ordering her to remain stationary or be destroyed. The indignity of being made to wait was only made worse by the fact it was her former ship that was doing the enforcing.

Adra had always hated living in space, subjected to the constant drone of starship engines and power conduits. But at least the powerful and advanced War Frigate had been well equipped, and had even afforded her a level of subdued luxury. The Destroyer-class battleship was dated and rudimentary in comparison, but at least Adra could take some solace from the fact its smaller engines produced a more tolerable drone.

"Clearance has been granted, Vice Provost," announced Vika, as the menacing form of the frigate began to power away. "We are to proceed to docking level alpha."

"Proceed, Adjutant Vika," said Adra from her position on the small command platform in the center of the bridge. It was a far cry from her lofty perch on the War Frigate. Gone was the halo of screens above her head, to be replaced by a single static screen on a pedestal to her right. And instead of rows of gleaming consoles crewed by dozens of simulants, there was only a single engineering control station and tactical console, in addition to the solo pilot's console. Vika was stationed alongside the pilot simulant and was responsible for all other ship's fuctions. The indignity of the situation had not been lost on Vika either; Adra had seen the disgusted look on her face the first time she had set foot on their new bridge.

Adra did not consider herself to be prideful, but she could not deny the profound shame she was experiencing at the reduction in her status and her humble new surroundings. That she was able to tolerate it at all was for one reason. Adjutant Vika's misjudged intervention in her tribunal, followed by Kagan assigning her to the Nexus, had provided the opportunity to finish what she had started. From staring defeat and death in the face, events had conspired to give her a second chance to destroy the humans – though this time it would be purely out of spite, and not to save her own reputation. The latter was in tatters, never to be repaired.

Adra again had to remind herself that she did not believe in fate, though it was becoming harder to accept that all the different strands that had led her to this moment were merely the work of chance.

Vika rested her hand onto the shoulder of the solo pilot simulant, one of only two active simulant crew required to operate the compact, timeworn vessel, and the ship began to accelerate towards the artificial planetoid. Vika watched as the frigate slipped off the edge of the viewport to give an unobstructed view of the Nexus behind it. The radiance from the system's yellow star reflected crisply off its slowly rotating shell, flickering like firelight reflected in metal.

"We will arrive on-station in five minutes, thirteen seconds," Vika added, glancing down at the small console on a pedestal to her side.

Adra did not reply, but continued to observe

her new adjutant closely. The act of resting her hand gently on the shoulder of the simulant, rather than knocking or nudging it into action as was the norm, was one of many traits that distinguished her new adjutant from others of her rank. Since Adra had assumed command of the Destroyer, Vika had executed each of her commands with the grace and elegance of a master of ceremonies, and had impressed in all areas of her duties. The similarities to Lux were almost nil; she lacked her brother's questioning nature and stuttering indecision. And although Lux had possessed fortitude enough to endure super-luminal travel, it was clear that in pure physicality Vika was by far his superior too. But, none of these traits were as important as loyalty to Adra. In the end, Lux had proven his worth, through a selfless dedication and belief in his commander – his superior. Even if they spent the next two decades together, Adra knew that Vika would never see her as superior or even equal to her. Resentment would grow, day by day and year by year. She wondered how long Vika could maintain her pretense of respect and follow Adra's commands, when under the surface she yearned to rip her throat out.

Vika attentively observed the pilot simulant as they entered the inner structure of the Nexus, passing through the airlock gate, before finally setting down with a vibrant clunk on their designated pad. "Docking complete. Proceeding to shut down and secure main engines," said Vika, tapping commands into her small screen, before turning to face Adra, hands pressed to the small of her back. "I await your orders, Vice Provost."

Adra was aware of the subtle and deliberate manner in which Vika always stressed the word, 'Vice' with added prominence. "Your orders are to follow me, Adjutant," replied Adra, stressing Vika's rank with a similar level of condescension, "and to stay out of my way."

"It would be my pleasure, Vice Provost," said Vika in a way that made it clear she would find no enjoyment in it whatsoever.

Adra held her eyes for a moment, willing Vika to make a more overt show of disrespect, but the Adjutant merely stared back, blankly. Adra silently cursed her and then turned and marched off the bridge, making the short walk to the rear cargo ramp that lead out into the docking bay. She noted the rhythmic thump of Vika's boots following behind, in perfect time with her own.

Adra was familiar with the layout of the Nexus, though she had not set foot on it for more than a century. The Nexus had been where Adra had completed her initial work on the human-simulant hybrids and also where she had first uploaded the control programs to the CoreNet. It operated autonomously for the most part and was unoccupied, save for a complement of Hedalt technicians from the scientific and engineering disciplines, who were its custodians. But the majority of functions were performed by a small army of lobotomized simulant workers who performed the regular and more laborious tasks.

Adra swept through the maze of corridors and sectors inside the vast complex and headed directly for her old research laboratory. Given the scale of the Nexus there was room enough for a thousand laboratories, and so she knew that her lab would have remained untouched, despite the passing of centuries.

As she continued, she again found herself admiring the simple, functional design of the Nexus. It was a masterful feat of engineering. An icosahedron over sixty kilometers in diameter at its widest point; it had operated tirelessly for eons. But the most remarkable aspect of the Nexus was its inexhaustible power source. At its core the Nexus harnessed a tear between normal space and the sub-layer that comprised the Fabric, sucking energy from one into the other. This not only gave it an unending source of power, but it was also the reason for its unique ability to connect directly with every super-luminal node in the galaxy, like neural pathways in a brain.

Adra reached the entrance to her old research and testing laboratory and pressed her hand to the security pad. A needle no larger than an eyelash shot out and pierced the center of her palm, drawing a small sample of her blood. Then a second later a white beam of light scanned across her face, before the large metal doors slid open with a hiss that allowed the older, staler air inside to bleed out. Adra entered, triggering the activation of power relays and computer consoles that had been dormant for hundreds of years. She could smell the ozone in the air as dusty circuits suddenly received power and lights blinked on all around the laboratory.

Vika followed, more cautiously than Adra, paying attention to each and every corner of the laboratory, which occupied a volume more than three times that of their Destroyer. A large section of the space was given over to an open chamber to the right of the door. Vika observed what looked like rows of stasis pods lining each side. The section to the left of the entrance was a far busier and more claustrophobic collection of smaller rooms surrounding a larger workshop. Adra had gone directly ahead into the largest of a group of glass-fronted rooms, which she assumed must have been Adra's personal office.

Since Adra had explicitly ordered her to stay out of her way, Vika decided to explore the open chamber to the right, stepping down a shallow flight of stairs to reach the chamber. Moving into the center she looked into each of the stasis pods, all of which were empty. Then she grasped the purpose of the space. Kagan had told her that Adra was responsible for the creation of the human-simulant hybrids, including the high-functioning Hunter simulant models. This laboratory space must have been where she had developed these simulant units – the prototypes for the cybernetic machines that now numbered in the billions, and without which their Empire could not properly function.

Vika paced to the end of the chamber, making sure to check inside each one of the pods, but all were empty – all except for a row of four at the very end of the chamber. These were set apart from the rest, standing up against the far wall, and were further distinguished from the others by a single console screen on a pedestal beside the far right pod. She moved closer and wiped away the thin layer of grime from the glass cases of each pod, instantly recognizing the simulant faces staring back from inside each. The first pod contained Tactical Specialist Blake Meade, the second Pilot Casey Valera, the third was Captain Taylor Ray and the fourth was Technical Specialist Satomi Rose. Vika stepped back, confused as to why only these four simulants remained, and why they had never been put into service. She quickly checked to make sure that Adra was still oblivious to her actions, and then moved in front of the console screen. It was misted with decades of dust and dirt, and she wiped it clean with a fold of her long, black coat, before tapping the screen twice to activate it. The console slowly glowed back to life and on the screen Vika saw a simple status readout of each unit. She read each entry in turn.

Blake Meade, Prototype A1:

Status - Non Viable. Neural activity, zero.

Casey Valera, Prototype A1:

Status - Non Viable. Neural activity, zero.

Taylor Ray, Prototype A1:

Status - Non Viable. Neural activity, zero.

Satomi Rose, Prototype A1:

Status – Viable. Unexplained neural activity.

SEVEN

The scout remained in the system for several hours, during which time all they could do was sit and wait. Taylor and the others didn't feel the cold, but the temperature quickly became uncomfortable for James, and Taylor had ordered him to don an environment suit. These suits were designed for limited space walks and hostile planetary environments. Considering that three of the four crew on the Contingency One were humanoid cyborgs with synthetic bodies, the fact that James appeared most out of place at his station on the bridge was testament to just how alien he looked.

"How are you doing over there, Technical Specialist?" asked Taylor, cheerfully, directing the question at the helmeted mass of material and metal, awkwardly perched on the seat at the mission ops station.

James raised an arm and gave a clumsy thumbs up, "I'm okay, Captain."

Blake, who was reclined back in his chair at tactical also lifted a hand, "We come in peace..." he said in a stilted accent, "Take us to your leader!"

Casey laughed and spun around in her chair once as an extension of her amusement. Then she stopped and suddenly acted all serious, "Wait, wouldn't his leader technically be Colonel Collins?"

Blake realized his error and feigned shock, "On second thoughts, don't take us to your leader," he added in the same stilted manner, "He's an asshole!"

Casey laughed and spun around again. Even the bulky suit containing James jostled up and down as he laughed inside its protective cocoon. Taylor smiled, but in the absence of Commander Sonner, felt he should do the 'captainly' thing and admonish Blake for his comment. "Okay, that's enough Tactical Specialist Meade. He may be an asshole, but he is our commanding officer. Let's keep it respectful."

"Whatever, Cap," said Blake, "you're the boss." Speaking these last few words out loud seemed to remind Blake of something, and he folded his arms, scowling. "I mean, technically *you're* the boss, right, Cap? 'Cos we ain't part of Earth Fleet, not really. Hell, we ain't even human!"

"Technically, yes," admitted Taylor, "but we're still partly human, and the original human versions of us were Earth Fleet officers."

"Yeah, but that's like sayin' my grandpa was in Earth Fleet, so that means I automatically am too," Blake argued back. "All I'm sayin' is that I don't think *we* need to be takin' orders from this Collins guy." Then he pointed to James, "Not like our extra-terrestrial friend over there has to."

Casey smiled at the joke, but refrained from laughing or spinning herself around in her chair; she knew that in his own special way, Blake was raising a serious point. Taylor glanced over at James and noted that his environment suit was no longer shuddering, meaning he was likely paying close attention too.

"We can't fight the Hedalt if we're fighting amongst ourselves, Blake," Taylor answered. "We need a command structure and he happens to be the most senior officer."

"Aw, c'mon, Cap, that's just political BS, an' you know it!" Blake hit back. "Why're we even fightin' this war for them? As that assh..." he caught himself just in time, but made it clear the correction was unwilling, "as Colonel Collins is so fond of remindin' you, we're not human. We're their former enemies, an' in case ya hadn't noticed, they don't like havin' us around."

Taylor had wondered how long it would be before Blake's pessimism and glass-half-empty attitude resurfaced, though in some ways it was comforting. It reinforced the fact that he was essentially the same Blake Meade he'd always known. But, he couldn't deny that he had a point too. Taylor's reasons for wanting to fight the Hedalt were his own, but the more he reconnected with his former crew, and the more the human population grew, the more obvious it had become that they didn't fit in. For him, the fight had become personal – it was about stopping Provost Adra, and rescuing Satomi. What would hopefully end up being Earth's last war was something he felt increasingly more detached from, but the training and instincts that were in his head from the original Captain Taylor Ray were hard to ignore. He still felt duty-bound to fight, but he also wanted to because it was the right thing to do. Leaving Sonner and the others to face Adra and the Hedalt alone seemed cowardly.

"Look, Blake, I understand where you're coming from, really I do," said Taylor, "and I'd be lying if I told you I hadn't wondered the same." He paused to take the measure of Blake's reaction, but the TacSpec officer didn't interrupt; he, like the others, was still hanging off his every word. "You're right; maybe this isn't our fight and it never was, but we're a part of this war, whether we like it or not. I don't like what the Hedalt did to me and you and Casey, or what they did to Earth. Someone has to even the score, and it might as well be us."

Blake mulled this over for a few seconds, while glancing over at Casey, whose soft smile and static expression weren't giving much away. Then he shook his head gently and looked back at Taylor, "Okay, Cap, if that's your call, I'll go with it." He opened his arms wide, gesturing to the dark, cold and near-silent interior of the bridge, "It's not like I got anythin' better to do!" Casey's smiled widened. Then the mission ops console bleeped an alert and everyone reacted instantly, darting over to check it.

"What is it?" asked Blake as they all peered down at the console.

James, despite the bulk of the environment suit, had already managed to analyze the alert. "It's another jump signature."

"In or out of the system?" asked Taylor.

"Hard to tell without fully powering up the sensors," James replied. "But that would make us a lot easier to spot, assuming the scout was still in the system."

Taylor rubbed the smooth synthetic skin on his cheek. He knew it was a risk, but they couldn't sit out in space forever. "Okay, take a peek, but make sure it's quick."

Blake leaned in towards Casey with a twinkle in his eyes, and then muttered in hushed tones, "That's what Satomi used to say to him..."

Casey rolled her eyes and jabbed him in the ribs, though she had to admit that was one of his better attempts at inuendo.

Remarkably, given his enhanced simulant hearing Taylor had been too preoccupied with the scan result to pick up on the comment. He watched eagerly as James finished the sensor sweep and then turned awkwardly towards him.

"No sign of the ship, Captain," said James, "but from the residual ion trail, it would suggest the ship was heading out of the system when it jumped."

Taylor, Casey and Blake exchanged relieved smiles, before Taylor placed a hand on James' shoulder, "Okay, power up, and then send a message to the other ships to do the same and return to base, smartly."

"Aye, Captain," said James, "I'll be glad to get out of this suit, I'm bursting for a pee."

"Too much information, Mr. Sonner," said Taylor, to stifled chortles from Casey and Blake behind him. "But, by all means, you are relieved so you can, well, relieve yourself." This set Blake and Casey off laughing uncontrollably, holding on to each other for support.

Just as James got up, the mission ops console

bleeped again, this time indicating an incoming message from the transmitter array on the moon's surface.

"Don't worry, I'll get it," said Taylor, pointing him towards the door. James gladly accepted the offer and ran off the bridge while Taylor put the message through onto the viewport.

"Captain, is everything okay?" asked a visibly concerned Commander Sarah Sonner, "We monitored rising power signatures up there, so I assume the ship you spotted has gone?"

"It's gone, Commander, but there's no way to know if it will come back," Taylor answered, "or if it will bring some friends if it does."

"I told you we should not delay!" snapped Collins, directing the statement more at Sonner than Taylor. "If the enemy knows our location, we must act now and deploy the fleet at once."

"I would have to agree, Commander," said Taylor, though the words tasted bitter in his mouth. "We might be compromised."

"Damn it!" said Sonner balling her hands into fists. "Okay, I agree," she added, grudgingly. "I still don't think we're ready, but it looks like our time is up. If the enemy finds this base and the fleet is still inside the lava tube, it could be the shortest battle in history."

"Good, finally some sense from all of you!" said Collins with a triumphant air of superiority. Taylor could see that Sonner was fighting hard not to shove one of her balled fists down his throat. "Order the four Nimrods out there with you to return for refueling and arming. And get back here yourselves."

"Aye, Colonel, the Nimrods are already en route," said Taylor, but he could see that Sonner was eager to interject.

"Captain, you've just been exposed to some extremely low temperatures for a prolonged period," Sonner cut in, "make sure you take a walk first. I need you to stretch your legs. We don't want your simulant frame to seize up."

Taylor noted that her eyes were unusually wide and that she kept waggling her eyebrows. "Commander, the temperature on the bridge didn't drop below about forty or so, which isn't too bad. And I feel fine..."

"Captain, that's an order," Sonner cut in. Collins was scowling at her, probably just as confused as Taylor. "Go for a walk. Perhaps take a look at the starlight..."

Taylor finally understood what she meant and felt foolish for not getting it sooner, "Oh, yes, okay Commander. Actually, I'd already had the same idea."

"Now is hardly the time for stargazing!" growled Collins. "Is this absolutely necessary?"

"The Commander is our foremost expert on

simulant technology, Colonel," said Taylor, getting into the part, "so I think we should do as she suggests."

"Just make it quick and then get back here," grumbled Collins. Then he turned to Sonner. "Start the evacuation, Commander. I want all ships ready to launch as soon as possible."

"Understood, Colonel," said Sonner, a little wearily, before glancing at Taylor and adding, "Enjoy your little walk, Captain. Contingency base, out."

The viewport faded to black just as the bridge door swung open and James entered, "Hey, what did I miss?"

"Nothin' much. Collins just ordered us to war, is all..." said Blake, casually. James felt doubly relieved that he'd just been to the restroom.

"James, do you know anything about simulant regeneration tech?" asked Taylor, swiftly changing the subject.

James shrugged, "Yes, Captain, a little. Sarah... I mean Commander Sonner, ran me through how it works, including how to monitor the connection to the CoreNet and set up the DMZ." Then his head drooped and his voice wilted a little. "She said it's best if more than one person knows how, in case, you know, anything happens."

"That's a bit morbid," said Taylor, recognizing the sudden change in James' mood, "but pragmatic too. And helpful, as it turns out."

"Helpful how, Captain?"

Taylor was not looking forward to the part that came next. "Because I need you to help me take a little walk..."

EIGHT

Taylor stood in front of the starlight door, trying to muster up the courage to walk through it. The resurgence of physical emotions while inside the Fabric still took him by surprise. *Being brave is a hell of a lot easier when you have a body that doesn't feel nervous...* he thought to himself.

However, despite the risk that Provost Adra was monitoring the CoreNet for signs of an 'anomaly', ready to purge Taylor from existence at any moment, he knew he had to step through and travel to Earth. At least this time he knew how to get there, because he'd already traveled along the threads of the Fabric to reach the super-luminal node the Hedalt had positioned in the Sol system. But he also remembered how quickly his incursion into the Fabric had been detected by Provost Adra, and so he knew the chances were high that she would find him again. He just had to hope he had time to gather enough information about the Hedalt forces before she did so.

He took a deep breath, stepped through the door and closed his eyes. "Earth..." he said out loud, picturing the blue orb in his mind, "take me to Earth."

Instantly he could feel his body moving, and he opened his eyes to see himself surging towards one of the countless translucent cubes spread across the galaxy. Before he knew it, he'd raced into the center and rapidly changed direction, like a pinball repelled by a bumper. He kept his eyes open as he sped through more cubes, trying to stay focused and alert, aware that if he blacked out he could be caught by Adra with no way to escape. But despite his efforts, he found his vision blurring and with each passing second it became more of a struggle to stay conscious.

Then, just as suddenly as his incredible journey along the threads of the Fabric had started, his rapid voyage through space ended and he was confronted by the unmistakable shimmering ball of blue that was the planet Earth. Wasting no time, he urged himself closer, until he was almost in orbit, but he didn't need to look hard to gather the reconnaissance he needed. Assembled in orbit, close to the super-luminal transceiver, was an intricate formation of dozens of ships, arranged into squadrons of five. Taylor swept closer, observing that each squadron contained at least one or two heavy cruisers that were many times larger than their own Nimrod-class cruisers. While some of the designs were new to Taylor, he recognized the War Frigates at once, and counted twenty before he stopped. Twenty frigates on their own would be a match for the Nimrod fleet, and this was only a fraction of the Hedalt force. All in, Taylor estimated that there were already more than a hundred ships protecting Earth, and although in pure numbers they had a force roughly equal in size, the reality was that the Nimrods didn't stand a chance. And there was nothing to say that more Hedalt ships weren't on the way.

"Taylor, quickly, we don't have much time!"

Satomi's voice came out of nowhere. Taylor jolted around, looking in all directions, but he couldn't see her. "Satomi? Where are..."

He hadn't even finished the sentence before he was moving again at super-luminal speeds, this time at even more dizzying velocities than before, but to where he had no idea. Cube after cube appeared and vanished and at each node Taylor was bounced this way and that, with each step adding to the stabbing pain in his head until the blur of light suddenly resolved. It took him a few moments to readjust, whereupon he found himself standing in a large open space with dark metal walls and coarse-grated decking. While his body appeared to be stationary his mind was still spinning.

"Taylor, I'm here!" he heard Satomi call out and he tried to focus, but the room continued to spin, as if the effect of one too many bourbons had just kicked in. Then he felt hands on his shoulders and heard the voice again, louder than before, "Taylor!" Suddenly Satomi was in front of him. He looked at her hands, resting on the sides of his shoulders and wondered how she could be touching him. But it wasn't the same as the physical press of solid matter; it was more like the electrical tingle of pure energy.

"I'm here, I'm okay," said Taylor, as Satomi's hands fell to her sides. With his head no longer spinning he could now see the room clearly. It was a large, empty hall with stasis pods lining the wall to either side. Satomi was standing several meters from the back wall, in front of another row of pods, and something else. He cocked his head to the side to look past Satomi and saw a tall figure in the unmistakable black armor of a Hedalt soldier.

Adra! Taylor thought, and then he called out, "Satomi, we have to go, that soldier..."

"That isn't who you think it is," Satomi interrupted, "but she's just as dangerous."

"We have to get out of here!" Taylor said, forgetting that he wasn't really in the room. The illusion of his body inside the Fabric and CoreNet was so real it was easy to forget that he only existed as thought and energy.

"She can't see or hear you, Taylor!" said Satomi, trying to reassure him, "I just need you to listen. It won't be long before they realize you're here. We may only have a minute, maybe less!"

Taylor nodded and tried to control his emotions, though the sight of the soldier was impossible to ignore. Satomi took Taylor's hand and instantly they were transported across the large room and into an office or small workshop of some kind.

"Look," said Satomi, pointing to a vast computer console screen that must have been a quarter the size of the entire viewport on the Contingency One, "This is where I am. Where you are now."

Taylor looked at the screen, which showed a roughly spherical object, possibly a space station, along with data readouts spread across twenty or more different areas of the screen. "Where, Satomi, what am I looking at?" he asked, panic causing his voice to rise half an octave.

Satomi took his hand again, which tingled like a vibrating tuning fork, and drew it towards the screen. "Here, look at the coordinates," Satomi said, "you'll have to remember them. Can you do that? I know that your memory for numbers hasn't always be great." Then she smiled, "Your head was always too full of quotes from old books."

Taylor smiled too; it was a unexpected moment that reminded him that Satomi was real – that she still knew him. He read the coordinates and began to repeat them over and over in his head. "How far is it?" Taylor asked, remembering that the Contingency One's jump range was limited, and that even with its upgraded computers the calculation speed was still sluggish.

"It's far, but you don't have to jump the threads to get here," said Satomi, and then she extended her arms and stretched them out towards the space around them, "This is the Fabric, Taylor. This is the Nexus. This is where the Fabric begins and ends. If you jump to those co-ordinates from any super-luminal node, there's a thread that always ends here. This is where they made us, Taylor, and to end the war this is where you must come."

"I'll always come for you, Satomi, I told you that," said Taylor, reaching for her and again feeling the static field repel their virtual forms.

"No, Taylor, not for me," said Satomi. "The Nexus controls every simulant in the galaxy. If you disable the Nexus, all of the simulants will cease to function. Billions of simulants, Taylor. Their space stations, mines, outposts and almost all of their starships will be crippled in an instant. They can't function without simulants. It's their strength, but also their Achilles heel."

"But if I disable the Nexus with you still inside?" said Taylor, unable to think of anything but rescuing Satomi, "Before, I wake you?"

"Then I'll cease to function too," said Satomi, "but you can't think about that, Taylor."

"Damn it, Satomi, if I can't save the one person I care most about then why the hell am I fighting at all?"

"You know why, Taylor," said Satomi, softly. "You can't place me above the survival of the human race. And if it came down to it, you know you wouldn't."

Taylor was furious, and the physical feeling of rage was impossible to ignore, "No, not this time. I don't care if I have to tear this Nexus apart with my bare hands, I won't leave it without you. I'd rather blow the damn thing to hell with you and me inside it!"

"How... romantic," said Satomi, and the darkly humorous response made them both laugh out loud, despite the nervous intensity of the situation.

But then Taylor started to feel pain building inside his temples. He winced and pressed his fingers to the source of the pain.

Satomi's voice hardened. "She's found you... you have to leave, now!"

Taylor stumbled back and tried to fight the pain, but it was hopeless, "How do I get inside?" he stammered, realizing he had no idea how he could possibly disable the Nexus.

"Leave that to me, Taylor," said Satomi, "just get here, I'll do the rest."

Taylor nodded, but this just made the pain inside his head even worse. Satomi reached up and held his head in her hands, helping to numb the pain. "Destroy the Nexus, Taylor. And if you can, find me too. Find me, Taylor..."

Then the touch of Satomi's hands was gone and Taylor was flying, out through the walls of the Nexus and into space. He briefly caught sight of the planet below; an ugly, gray world that was blanketed in a surface-wide industrialized city. And then he was moving again, bouncing through the nodes. The pain continued to grow and Taylor cried out, trying to release some of the pressure, but it was like a vice was slowly and relentlessly tightening around his skull. Then he was inside the deep space corridor with the starlight door mere meters in front of him. He scrambled towards it but fell prone as the pain spread to every part of his body. It felt like he was being crushed and torn apart at the same time. He inched forward, but soon he could no longer move his feet or hands, and the immobility was spreading along his body, towards his core. Eventually he was within centimeters of the threshold, but he could not move any further. He yelled out, "James!... James, help!" but there was no answer. Putting everything he had left into one last burst, he managed to lurch forward just far enough that the tips of his fingers passed over the glowing barrier between the Fabric and the safe space beyond. And then the pain swallowed him whole and he passed into nothingness.

NINE

Vika felt a strange sensation creep across her skin, as if she'd been exposed to a static charge. She shivered and patted down the affected areas, but then the sensation quickly dissipated, leaving her feeling puzzled and disquieted. She didn't have time to dwell on it, though, as a low pulsing alert sounded from the other end of the chamber. This drew her attention away from the strange occurrence and also gave her an excuse to finally find out what Adra had been doing. She quickly covered the length of the room, leaving the stasis pods containing the four prototype high-functioning simulants behind, and entered the suite of offices without knocking or otherwise requesting entry.

"I thought I told you not to disturb me?"

complained Adra, as Vika entered the room.

"Apologies, Vice Provost, but I heard what sounded like an alert and felt it prudent to investigate," said Vika, unperturbed by Adra's passive-aggressive stance. She did not fear Adra, and after more than five years serving High Provost Kagan, she was comfortable standing her ground in the company of those who would intimidate others of her age and rank.

"It is none of your concern," Adra replied, continuing to focus on the console screens. "Return to the ship and prepare for launch."

Vika was far enough inside the office that she could see the information spread across the wall of screens to the rear, and it did not take her long to work out what had caused the alert. "You have already completed work on the new signal trace program," she said, the surprise evident in her voice. She quickly scanned the other screens, "And there has been another incursion. You appear to have traced the source already."

Adra turned and peered at Vika through narrowed eyes, "How do you know this?"

"I was a member of the scientific division, before participating in the trials to compete for the position of Adjutant to the High Provost," said Vika. "I focused mainly on starship design, but I am also familiar with your earlier work on human-simulant hybrids."

Adra would have normally reviewed the record of her adjutant in detail, but events since the tribunal had moved quickly, and she had neglected to study Vika's file. That she had transitioned from a scientific discipline to Warfare Command, as Adra had done, was worthy of respect, but that she had also succeeded in the trials to become Adjutant to the High Provost made the achievement doubly impressive. But she also pitied Vika for allowing her emotions and desire for vengeance to interfere with her career. She could have become one of the youngest provosts in history. Now, like Adra, the best she could hope for was to attain the rank of vice provost and to remain always just outside the inner circle of influence. For someone of her abilities and youth, to be cursed with such a mediocre existence was a waste, but also perhaps a just reward for her meddling.

"You are correct, Adjutant Vika," said Adra, curious to learn how Vika would react once she realized what her next move would be. "I had already completed work on the detailed signal trace while awaiting the start of the tribunal." Vika wondered why she had not mentioned this to High Provost Kagan at the time, but knew better than to openly question Adra's judgment. "And, as I knew it would, the rogue simulant has entered the Fabric once again."

"You have its precise location?"

"I do," Adra replied, though she chose to omit the detail that the location was a star system she was already familiar with, because she had been there before. The trace had pinpointed the location as the second moon of the fourth planet of the system she had visited after first learning of the anomaly. It was where a Hunter Corvette had gone missing, supposedly crashed on the surface. But it seemed the humans had been more cunning than she'd given them credit for. That she had come so close to discovering their base so long ago irked her, and she did not want Vika to be aware of this failure. But, she vowed she would not fail again. "The purge did not have time to complete, but it is proof enough that the new trace works. Should it attempt to enter the Fabric again, I will be able to locate and eradicate it swiftly."

"This news is significant," replied Vika, feeling that perhaps such a success might go some way to restoring their fortunes with Kagan. "At your order, I shall communicate this discovery to Warfare Command."

"No," replied Adra firmly, "you will not communicate anything of this to Warfare Command or the High Provost directly. Return to the ship and begin calculations. We jump to the system at once."

Vika held her ground, "High Provost Kagan

expressly ordered that any discovery be reported to him without delay."

"High Provost Kagan is no longer your concern, Adjutant Vika," sneered Adra. "You will do as *I* command. And you will do it now."

Vika still did not flinch. She was aware of the consequences of disobeying a command from a direct superior, but she had also heard Kagan's express command that he be informed without delay. Perhaps as a full provost, Adra would be permitted some leeway to go beyond her orders – leeway that she had vastly exceeded in the past – but as Vice Provost she had no such flexibility. To communicate with Warfare Command behind Adra's back would be seen as dishonorable, but she could still refuse the command. It was a risk, as there was no guarantee that the Warfare Council would consider her defiance justified. And if they did not, Vika would be the next to face Tribunal, and likely execution. Vika made her choice. She would not blindly follow Adra as her brother had done, at the cost of his life.

"No, Vice Provost," Vika said, "I will not comply. Our orders from the High Provost contain no ambiguity. I will not defy them."

Adra realized she had been wrong about Vika; she was not going to meekly obey and do her duty as her brother had done. Adra knew that Vika had a valid reason to dispute her order. And she also knew that Warfare Command would most likely side with her, given recent events. But by disobeying her superior, Vika would have to survive Adra's judgment first. In some ways she respected Vika's choice to fight rather than kowtow to her orders – at least it would settle their feud, rather than both of them enduring what could be decades of mutual resentment.

"You are refusing my command, Adjutant Vika?" asked Adra, calmly.

"I am," replied Vika, with equal poise.

There was nothing more to say, at least not with words, and so Adra's next response was with action. She rushed towards Vika, and though the Adjutant had expected an attack, she was still caught on the back foot by Adra's ferocious speed. A fist hammered into Vika's chin, but she managed to partially block the next blow, more out of instinct than intent. Adra then spun and thrust a kick to Vika's chest. The power of the blow sent Vika crashing through the glass wall of the office, peppering her with razor-sharp shards that pricked and scraped her face and neck. Adra surged after her and tried to stomp her heel down on Vika's throat, but she rolled to the side, feeling the glass bite deeper into her flesh. Ignoring the pain, Vika flashed out a leg, sweeping Adra to the deck. Both soldiers were back on their feet in a second, glass fragments studded into their armor like shimmering dragon scales.

Adra advanced again, fists, elbows and kicks flying, but Vika blocked the attacks and countered with a thumping knee to Adra's gut. Adra staggered back and soaked up a follow-up combo, but Vika had underestimated Adra's resilience. Deflecting the next attack, Adra countered with a cross that sent Vika reeling out towards the chamber containing the stasis pods.

Adra's next attack was telegraphed and Vika dodged, countering with a kick to the back of Adra's knee. The Vice Provost dropped and an elbow landed hard to the side of her face. A shard of glass embedded into Vika's armor gouged a bloody furrow across Adra's cheek. She grimaced and grabbed Vika's arm, before launching her into an empty stasis pod, shattering more glass, which poured over her face and inside the collar of her armor. Like a boxer hemmed into a corner, Adra pummeled Vika to body and face, cracking armor, bone and knuckles, before Vika finally managed to wrestle her away and push her back.

Vika spat out bloodied, broken teeth and grabbed Adra's armored jacket, and despite the Vice Provost's greater stature and strength, Vika's rage overcame her. She threw Adra to the deck, pinned her and rained down frenzied punches to her face and head. But her ill-discipline would cost her. Adra caught Vika's wrists and rose a knee up to her gut, breaking the pin before kicking the Adjutant away.

Again, both were on their feet in a second. Both were cut and bloodied and broken, and as much as Adra hated to admit it, Vika had so far matched her almost blow-for-blow.

"You fight well, for one so young," said Adra, circling around her opponent. Despite the nature of the words, the tone was condescending, not complimentary.

"The fight is not over yet..." replied Vika, mirroring Adra move for move. She spat blood onto the deck and wiped her mouth with the back of her hand. "But before I kill you, I'll make you suffer for what you did to Lux."

Adra smiled. Vika was strong and perhaps even her equal in combat, but she was also emotional and this gave Adra the advantage.

"I did nothing. Lux died because he was weak," Adra hit back, "Weak and worthless, just as you have become." Vika bristled, and almost charged, but just managed to rein in her rising fury. Adra knew she had touched a nerve and continued to press her, "But even if his weakness had not killed him, I would have done it myself out of pity!"

Vika screamed and charged at Adra in a feverish attempt to tackle her to the deck, but the attack was rushed and clumsy, and it gave Adra the opportunity she needed. She stooped, lowering her center to stop Vika from taking her down and then grabbed her head and cranked her neck, before spinning her into a choke hold. Realizing the danger she was in, Vika pushed back, ramming Adra into another empty stasis pod, but Adra held firm, adding pressure to the hold as more glass scratched their faces. Vika continued to fight, slipping a hand between Adra's arm and her neck, desperately trying to relieve the pressure on her carotid artery, while pounding elbows into Adra's side, but still the pressure increased, until Adra could feel Vika's strength failing and her efforts to break free become feeble and useless.

But then, without warning, Adra released her hold and pushed Vika away. She fell hard, driving the shards of glass further into her face and scalp, and tried to push herself up, but she only managed to rise to one knee before Adra was standing above her and drawing her serrated, black blade. It was only now, with Vika defeated, that honor would permit her to draw the weapon. While the blade was a fitting weapon to dispatch racketeers and the unworthy, a contest between members of the military elite was always settled hand-to-hand. A contest of pure strength and skill, as well as guile. A contest Adra had won.

"Submit," growled Adra through labored breaths, angling the tip of the blade towards Vika's throat. "I do not want you dead."

Vika spat more blood and then peered up into Adra's intense green eyes, "I would rather die than submit to you."

"You can die here, on your knees, gutted like a racketeer," said Adra, "or you can swear allegiance to me, and help me to finish what Lux could not."

"Don't speak his name!" Vika snarled back. "He was a fool to follow you. And you are a fool if you believe Kagan needs us. We are nothing!"

"I knew I was nothing the moment Kagan boarded my ship," snarled Adra, and the admission took Vika aback. "He took everything, from both of us! But I will not live out my days reduced to a shell of what I was."

"That is your choice, coward," growled Vika. "I will do my duty."

"You already broke your oath of duty by defying me, yet you believe that Kagan may yet give you another chance?" Adra laughed, contemptuously. "And you call me a fool!"

"I cannot betray Warfare Command!"

"Kagan already betrayed you!" Adra hit back, her voice rising to a shout, "He will never forgive your interference at the tribunal. He will ensure you suffer for that slight, right up until your miserable, pointless death." Then she became more urgent, almost pleading with Vika, "Join me, as Lux would have done. You can live a half-life, always less than what you were born to be, or together we can destroy this human threat. That is something Kagan can never take from you."

"And then what?" said Vika, "We destroy these humans and Kagan somehow doesn't find and kill us both. What comes after?"

Adra slid her knife back into it scabbard and stretched out a hand to Vika, "Then if you still want revenge against me for Lux, I will give you your chance again."

Vika remained on one knee, processing everything that Adra had said. She wanted to believe that continuing to do her duty would redeem herself in the eyes of Kagan and the other Provosts, but she knew Kagan as well as anyone alive, and she knew in her heart that Adra was right. Kagan was controlling and spiteful, and he would never forgive her. She was destined only for a life of mediocrity, forever to remain in the shadow of weaker and less capable soldiers. To believe she could be content with a life such as that was a lie she was now waking up to. Only the prospect of revenge against Adra had driven her on, but she had issued her challenge and failed. And though High Provost Kagan may have destroyed her life, he had not yet stripped her of honor.

"I will give you my allegiance," said Vika, extending her hand towards Adra, who took it and hoisted her to her feet. They stood, eye to eye, each with broken bones, angry gashes, dark bruises, and glass that sparkled inside their flesh like jewels. "But only until we destroy the humans, or fail in the attempt. Then, if we are both still alive, you and I will face each other again. And next time, I will kill you."

TEN

Taylor could hear someone shouting, but the voice seemed distant, as if he was hearing it through a stone wall. He blinked, but all he could see was a wall of light speckled with a chaotic pattern of blacks and greys, like an ancient de-tuned television set.

"Taylor!"

This time the shout was cleaner and more distinct, but he couldn't tell who it was, or even if it was a male or female voice. He tried moving his arms, which he had a vague sensation of still being attached to, but then felt someone holding them and pressing them back down. He tried to speak, but although a noise came out, it was just a garbled, nonsensical gibberish.

"We have to do something!" he heard a voice

say. "Contact your sister!"

"There's no time, his neural pathways are about to collapse!" shouted another voice. "The interfaces didn't reset to his normal waking status after I yanked him from the Fabric."

"Then plug him back in," said another voice, calmer, deeper, "Maybe it'll act like a reset button, y'know?"

"Will that work?"

"I have no idea, this tech is way beyond my understanding."

"Well, it's better than us just bawlin' at each other and watchin' him die, ain't it?"

"Okay, I'll try it," said the second voice again, "I'll use Sarah's DMZ program. It engages the neural interfaces in a similar way to the CoreNet."

"I'm going in too."

"Hey, wait a damn minute!" protested the deeper voice, "We don't know what that could do to you. This could be like a computer virus or somethin', and infect you too."

"I'm going in, Blake. He risked everything for us, and we should do the same."

"Hell, let me go then!"

"No, I'm going," the first voice replied, "I'll need you to pull me out if things go wrong."

"Whatever you're doing, do it fast!"

"Damn it, okay, but you'd better come back outta there, or I'm gonna be pissed!"

There was a sort of muffled laughter, but then the sounds became muddied again, and the fuzzy wall of light started to become even more chaotic. Taylor could feel himself losing touch with his senses and what little sensation there was in his body. And then, as if someone had flipped a switch, the noise and the lights disappeared and the next thing he knew he was standing in the cargo hold of the Contingency One. The rear ramp was lowered, exposing the star-studded vacuum of deep space, and standing in front of the opening, silhouetted by the glowing red sun beyond, was Casey Valera.

"Captain, are you okay?" shouted Casey, running over to him and grabbing his shoulders. Taylor felt the pressure of her touch, as real as the real world ever had felt.

"Yeah, I think so, Casey," said Taylor, now not only aware of the pressure of Casey's touch, but also of a growing pain behind his eyes. It was like someone had shoved a kebab skewer through his temples and was jostling it back and forth. "What happened?"

"James said that they hit you with the 'purge', whatever that is," said Casey, "you were trapped, part in and part out of the CoreNet, and he had to pull your consciousness out by force."

"I take it that didn't go so well?" Taylor replied, managing a little sarcasm despite the danger and precariousness of his situation.

Casey laughed, appreciating Taylor's ability to remain in good humor, "Not so great, no. But then we shunted your mind back into this DMZ place that Commander S cooked up, and... here we are."

"Why are you here?" asked Taylor, massaging his temples.

"Charming..."

"I'm sorry." Taylor realized how rude he sounded; the sharpness of the pain in his head had ironically caused him to become blunt. "I mean why are you also in the DMZ with me?"

"I don't know, I just thought it might help," said Casey, releasing Taylor's shoulders and shrugging her own, "like how this place helped to get my head straight when you unplugged me, and Blake too. I thought perhaps you could lean on me; you know, help share the burden."

"Smart thinking, Casey," said Taylor, managing a tepid smile.

"Well, I always was the brains of the outfit," said Casey, "and also the muscle, and the getaway driver, and the charming mastermind." Taylor frowned – the pain meant he'd barely heard her last few words – but Casey just patted him affectionately on the chest, "Never mind, Cap."

"So, what now?"

"I have no idea," said Casey freely, but also in a carefree way that made the bleak nature of the response sound like it wasn't an issue at all. "I guess we just hang here for a while until James figures it out." Then she wandered over to the open cargo bay door and sat down, letting her legs stretch down the ramp, like she was literally perched on the edge of the universe.

As Casey walked away the pain intensified, so Taylor quickly hurried over and sat down next to her. As soon as he did so, the stabbing sensation in his temples faded a little. "Well, as places to 'hang' go, this could be worse," he said, looking out towards the warm red sun, which was the centerpiece of their spectacular setting.

For a time they just sat in silence and enjoyed the view, and as they waited, Taylor began to feel the pain inside his head continue to slowly ebb away. The release of pressure allowed him to think straight again, and he started to go over everything Satomi had told him. For the briefest moment he panicked, believing he'd forgotten the co-ordinates she had shown him, but then they popped back into his head and he breathed a sigh of relief.

"Everything a'okay, Cap?" said Casey, hearing the sudden gasp. She was waggling sparkling yellow sneakers, and Taylor wondered if they were actually a real pair that she had owned, or just a mental projection of the footwear she fancied wearing at that moment.

"Yes, I'm actually starting to feel better, I think," he answered, pulling his eyes away from the waggling shoes and up to her eyes, which were looking back at him; concerned, but also strangely reassuring. "I found her, Casey."

"Satomi?" said Casey, excited. "You know where she is?"

"Yes, and the real kicker is that she's exactly where we need to go," said Taylor. "It's crazy, isn't it? Makes you wonder if there's someone pulling the cosmic strings after all."

"Or the cosmic threads," said Casey. She paused, then explained, in case Taylor hadn't quite followed her. "Threads like in the Fabric, I mean."

"I got it, Casey," said Taylor, giving her a gentle nudge with his shoulder, "My brain isn't that far gone... yet."

Casey laughed and nudged him back. For a time they watched the stars again in silence, but the void was soon filled by thoughts of Satomi. "I want Satomi to see this too," said Taylor, somberly. "I want us to be together." Then he hastily corrected himself, "All of us I mean... To be a full crew again."

Casey smiled, "It's okay, Cap, we all know how you feel about her." Taylor's cheeks flushed red, a tell his simulant body would have hidden, but he didn't try to deny it. Then Casey annunciated in a highly theatrical manner, "Love is like a friendship caught on fire..."

Taylor raised his eyebrows, "You know, I actually haven't heard that quote before. Who is it by?"

"Bruce Lee," said Casey, raising her guard as if ready to fight.

"Who?"

Casey rolled her eyes. "Never mind..." then she shot him a knowing wink, "If Blake were here, he'd actually have known that one."

Taylor snorted, "I'm surprised he didn't gallantly offer to babysit me in here instead of you," said Taylor.

"Oh, he did," said Casey, nonchalantly, "but, you're my Captain, and it's my job to steer you home safely."

Taylor's smile widened, and for a moment it was like nothing else existed in the universe but himself and Casey. There were no wars, no Hedalt, no threats or worries. Just two people who shared a bond that traversed space and time.

"No-one could do it better than you, Casey," said Taylor. "I'll always need you to steer me home."

Casey gave him another gentle nudge with her shoulder, "Aye, aye, Captain Taylor Ray."

ELEVEN

Taylor and Casey had barely emerged from the DMZ when Colonel Collins burst into the workshop on the Contingency One, closely followed by Commander Sonner, who was staring at the back of Collins' head with dagger eyes. But once she saw that Taylor and Casey were okay, her expression softened.

"What on Earth did you think you were doing, Captain?!" yelled Collins, addressing Taylor specifically. "I ordered you to return to base, not use this ability of yours to venture off into... wherever the blazes you just were!"

Blake who had immediately gone to check on Casey, leaned in closer so he could whisper into her ear. "Did that guy really just say, 'wherever the blazes', or have my ears gone funny?"

"Yeah, he said it," replied Casey, and then she smirked at him "And your ears are kinda funny."

Blake recoiled slightly and clasped hands over his ears, "Why, what's the matter with 'em?" Then Casey laughed and suddenly the room fell silent.

"Is there something amusing, Pilot Valera and Tactical Specialist Meade?" asked Collins, his eyes flicking between them, "or do simulants find the idea of risking all of our lives and the fate of the human race comical? I should have you all deactivated at once!"

Taylor positioned himself between Collins and Blake, before Blake could say or do something they would all regret. "I apologize, Colonel, I take full responsibility. My crew was only following my orders. It was our last and only chance to gather some intel on the Hedalt defenses around Earth, and I felt it was worth the risk."

Taylor's apology and detached professionalism seemed to deflate the growing bubble of anger inside Collins, at least enough that he forgot about Blake and Casey. But he was still red-faced and not done admonishing him, "That was not your decision to make. As long as you wear the Earth Fleet uniform, you follow my orders!"

But before Taylor could get in another word, Commander Sonner interjected, asking the only question that actually mattered, "What did you find out, Captain?"

Taylor met Sonner's eyes and she didn't need him to answer the question to know it was bad. She nodded and then folded her arms, before stepping alongside Collins. She didn't know how he'd react, but she needed to concentrate on remaining calm and unemotional to make sure that whatever Taylor told them was met with rational thinking, at least from her.

"It's bad news, Commander," said Taylor, and then he redirected his silver eyes on the Colonel's dilated pupils. "I wasn't able to hang around Earth for long, but I'd estimate there to be at least a hundred ships already stationed in high orbit, close to the super-luminal transceiver the Hedalt positioned near the planet."

"That doesn't sound like bad news, Captain," said Collins, huffily. "We also have a hundred ships, and I believe our stronger desire to win gives us the advantage!"

"It's not the number of ships that's the problem, Colonel," Taylor went on, "their vessels are far more powerful. I counted at least twenty of the War Frigates Sonner and my crew encountered, and each of those is worth two or three Nimrods just on their own. The rest of the fleet was comprised of larger and more advanced ships too, and there's no telling how many more Warfare Command have yet to amass at Earth."

"We have only your word on that, Captain,"

Collins hit back, "And for all I know, you could still be acting on behalf of the enemy, feeding us false information and outright lies."

"Colonel, let's be real," Sonner cut in, "if Taylor wanted to destroy us, he could have leveled this base with the Contingency One a hundred times by now." Collins' eyes narrowed, but Sonner's argument was hard to dispute. "I've seen what the Captain can do inside the CoreNet. If he says their fleet outmatches ours then we need to take him seriously." There was none of the prickly combativeness or condescension that usually characterized Sonner's conversations with Collins, only a cold solemnity that even the Colonel could not deny. The white-haired officer's expression darkened and he suddenly looked a decade older than his already-advanced years. He stepped back from Taylor, while rubbing a finger across the top of his mustache like a comb.

"Even if what you say is true, Captain, it changes nothing," said Collins after a deathly silence fell over the workshop for several seconds. "We cannot stay here, as we know this location is compromised. And we cannot return to the asteroid base or the reserve base. In short, we cannot retreat, and so the only direction we can go is forward. We must press the attack."

Remarkably, given that tense situations usually brought out the worst in Collins, Sonner thought that this was the most sane suggestion the Colonel had yet had. But it was also still the wrong decision. Sonner looked across to Taylor, hoping that his spacewalk had also uncovered some good news – something new that they could use – and she could see in his silver eyes that he still had something significant to add.

"We do have another option, Colonel," said Taylor, and immediately he had his complete attention. "In addition to my reconnaissance of Hedalt fleet strength around Earth, I was able to confirm a hypothesis that Commander Sonner and I have been working on." He glanced at Sonner, hoping she would take the hint and roll with it. The last thing he needed right now was to have to explain to Collins that the ethereal form of a simulant that was still plugged into the Hedalt system had been secretly passing information to him, like a modern day Virginia Hall. "I have uncovered the location of something the Hedalt call, 'the Nexus'." Taylor continued, still with the entire room hanging off his every word. "The Nexus is the central node of the entire simulant network. Its brain, so to speak, but also its heart. If we destroy the Nexus, we disable every simulant on every Warfare Command ship in the entire galaxy."

"It would cripple them, Colonel," Sonner cut in, following Taylor's lead, breathless excitement tainting her words. "It would nullify their advantage, rendering their bigger ships useless and inoperable. We know that even the huge War Frigates only have two Hedalt crew, which is too few to effectively operate a ship of that size. Without simulants we take away the advantage of their ships and technology. Hell, the odds may even tip in our favor!"

"And you say you know where this Nexus is?" asked Collins. He sounded skeptical, but Taylor and Sonner had piqued his interest nonetheless.

"I do, but it's deep in enemy territory, and it's big too. I mean, big like the size of a small moon," replied Taylor.

"Then how do you propose to destroy it?!" snapped Collins, seizing the first opportunity to criticize the plan. "We can't risk sending the fleet into enemy territory to destroy a planet-sized space station on the say-so of one simulant!"

Sonner gritted her teeth and stepped forward. Taylor could have handed Collins an 'off switch' for the entire Hedalt armada and he would still have contended the effort of pressing the button was too great. He was set on his plan, and it seemed that nothing was going to change his mind. "Colonel, it doesn't need the entire fleet," Sonner said, trying to retain her dispassionate delivery, but she was almost pleading with him to see sense, "Taylor can take the Contingency One. He knows how to disable this Nexus, isn't that right Captain?" She looked at Taylor hopefully, assuming that he wouldn't have brought up the Nexus if he didn't have a plan to take it down.

"Yes, I can do it," said Taylor, confidently. He wasn't sure where this new confidence had come from, since he had no idea how exactly to execute the plan, but he trusted Satomi, and Satomi had said she could get them inside.

"No, it's lunacy!" Collins hit back. "One ship against a space station is folly. We need every ship on the front line!"

"Colonel, if you'd just listen..." Sonner began, but Collins cut her off.

"No, no more talk of the Nexus or lone ships heading into enemy space!" Collins barked. "For all I know, it's just an excuse to run home to their Hedalt masters!"

Now it was Taylor who was at serious risk of throttling the Colonel where he stood. His intransigence defied logic and appeared to be solely due to his irrational prejudice against Taylor's simulant form.

"The original plan stands," Collins barked, "Is that clear?"

"Yes, Colonel," said Sonner, smartly, before anyone else in the room, including Taylor, could argue or complain further. "I'll make sure the Contingency One is refueled and ready, in time to launch with the rest of the fleet."

Taylor was surprised at Commander Sonner's sudden obedience, but a sly sideways look across to him suggested she was just paying lip service.

"Good, see to it, Commander," said Collins. "Report to me once preparations are complete." He then bustled out of the room again, but not before giving each one of the simulants a contemptuous look, as if they were convicted criminals. The door to the workshop slid shut and another deathly calm fell over the room.

"That guy is a grade-A asshole," grumbled Blake, breaking the silence. Then he turned to Taylor, "So, when do we leave, Cap?"

Taylor smiled and then met Sonner's eyes, "Permission to disobey orders, Commander?"

"Permission granted, Captain," said Sonner, "but I can't come with you on this one, I'm afraid. I need to stay here, and make sure Collins doesn't screw us over any more than he already plans to."

"I understand," said Taylor. Then he smirked, "so long as you don't mind me sitting in your command chair?"

"It was never mine, Captain; I just borrowed it for a while," Sonner replied. Then, with a heartfelt sincerity, she added. "The Contingency One is yours, Captain. It always was and it always will be. So long as you're feeling up to it?"

Taylor shrugged, "I feel fine, as far as this body

can feel anyway. I don't know what your DMZ program did, but it worked."

"You were lucky James dumped you in there," said Sonner, "and Casey going in with you was reckless, but luckily also the right call. The DMZ allowed your neural interfaces to reset, and somehow sharing the space with Casey's neural pattern speeded up their repair." Then she shrugged and threw her hands out to the side, "I don't know how or why, and honestly that bugs me. I'd love to study your brains some more."

"There ain't no way you're getting inside my head, lady," grunted Blake.

Casey scoffed, "What's to study? There's nothing in there but sawdust."

Taylor laughed as Blake jostled Casey with his shoulder. Sonner rolled her eyes and continued, "What I do know is that if you'd been exposed to that purge for a few seconds longer there would have been nothing left of you to save."

"Well, I don't plan on going back in any time soon," said Taylor, "It would be like willingly sticking my head inside a lion's mouth."

"But without your little 'party trick', how do you plan on getting inside the Nexus?" asked Sonner.

"Honestly, I haven't quite worked that one out yet," admitted Taylor, "But I've been promised some help when we get there."

Sonner frowned at the cryptic response, but then Blake stepped forward and coughed loudly to get their attention, "I hate to be the one makin' sense around here," he began, "but when we launch with the fleet an' Collins sees we're headin' someplace other than where he tells us, I don't trust him not to blow us outta the sky."

"I guess we'll just have to rely on Casey's ace piloting again," suggested Taylor, but Casey was shaking her head.

"I can dodge three or maybe four ships easy enough, Cap," said Casey, "but not ninety-nine."

"We don't need to dodge 'em," said Blake, "we just need someone willin' to get in the way long enough for us to make the jump. A sorta wingman. Even Collins ain't crazy enough to shoot through one of his own."

Taylor rubbed his chin, "We don't know these crews well enough to find someone willing to do that. Or who we could really trust. The esteemed commander aside, the human crew seem to look at us with a mix of fear and suspicion, no doubt thanks to Collins. "

"I have an idea about that," said Sonner, matching Taylor's earlier mystery, "but it means me making peace with an old friend."

TWELVE

Sarah Sonner entered the flight crew ready room and nervously scanned her eyes across the different tables and recreation areas until she saw the person she was looking for. She smoothed the creases out of her uniform jacket with the clammy palm of her hand and then adjusted her hair, before sucking in a long breath and letting it out slowly. "Okay, Sarah, here goes nothing..."

Sonner strode confidently over to a table with four flight crew sitting around it, drinking coffee while chatting and joking. The table fell silent as Sonner appeared in front of them.

A man wearing Captain's rank insignia initially looked like he'd seen a ghost, but then abruptly stood up and called out, "Crew, attention!" The other three pushed out their chairs and stood rigidly, all looking at Sonner.

"Sit down, all of you," said Sonner making a sort of pushing gesture with her hands, as if she was directing an invisible force that was pressing them down into their seats again. Then she looked at the Captain and said, "You know I don't go in for all that formality crap, Reese."

"I know," said the captain, "but I wouldn't want you to think I don't take my responsibilities and commitments seriously now, would I?"

"Oh, hell, really?" said Sonner, "We're just going to go straight into this? Don't you want to introduce me to your crew first?" Then she waved at the others, "Hi, I'm your Captain's ex-wife and we hate each other's guts."

The other three flight crew looked at each other awkwardly and then almost in perfect unison peered across to their Captain, in what was obviously a plea for help.

"Take five, everyone," said Reese, casually wafting a hand towards them, "the Commander obviously needs me for something," then he added, snippily, "for a change..."

Sonner laughed and shook her head, but the other crew were more than happy to accept Reese's invitation to scarper, and they all did so sharply, without a second look back at either Sonner or their Captain. Once they were safely out of earshot, Reese turned back to Sonner and threw up a stiff salute, "Captain Reese Turner, reporting for duty, sir."

"Knock it off, Reese, I have something serious to talk to you about," said Sonner, dragging one of the chairs away from the table and sitting down.

"Serious is all there is to talk about these days," said Reese, lowering the salute and them himself into his seat. But whereas Sonner sat upright and alert, as if she was sitting an exam, Reese relaxed, resting one arm over the back of the chair.

"I'm sorry I didn't come to see you earlier," said Sonner looking down at her hands, which were bundled together on the table.

"It's okay, Sarah, I know you've been a little pre-occupied," Reese replied, his voice now lacking the acid bite it had earlier. "Everyone on this base knows what you've done for us. You're quite the celebrity, in fact. My crew nearly peed their pants when they saw you marching over."

Sonner smiled, "Well, I'm glad they didn't."

"You and me both," said Reese, returning the smile. He leaned forward and rested his arms on the table, so that his hands were only a few centimeters from Sonner's. "So, what's up, Sarah? Even though there are only a few hundred humans left alive, you must still be pretty desperate if I'm the person you've turned to."

"Come on, Reese, you'd be the one person I turned to if there were still ten billion humans alive," Sonner replied, annoyed by how easily he was willing to start a fight. The heel of her foot was tapping uncontrollably on the deck plating. "And you know it."

"Really?" said Reese, with mock surprise. "Not your new simulant companion? What's his name again? Taylor Ray? Sounds like a superstar wrestler if you ask me..."

Sonner cocked her head and relaxed back in her chair, mirroring Reese's earlier casual stance, "Seriously? You're jealous of a robot?"

"It's the jilted party's prerogative to be jealous of their ex-partner's new squeeze..."

"Really, Reese, we don't have time for this..."

"If not now, then when, Sarah?" Reese cut in, suddenly far more earnest, but there was also anger close beneath the surface. "The world already ended once, and both of us dodged that bullet. But even if we win this battle, not all of us will make it."

"That's why I'm here, Reese," said Sonner, again leaning towards him and placing her hands on his. "There's a way we can even the odds, perhaps even flip them in our favor." Then she winced, "but it means not *exactly* obeying orders."

Reese laughed and leaned back again, pulling his hands out from underneath Sonner's, "Not conforming is your specialty, Sarah. But, I'm just glad to hear you do need me after all."

"It was your choice to take the promotion, Reese," said Sonner, starting to lose her patience, and her temper. "We both agreed to leave Earth Fleet, but it was your choice to stay. All our plans, our dreams – this new life we both wanted – you walked out on it. You left me first, Reese."

"Damn it, Sarah, but I came back," Reese snapped. "You'd already had a career and made Captain. You'd already got what you wanted out of Earth Fleet. I didn't want to leave and then always regret passing up a shot at the big chair. You'd think I blamed you, and part of me would always be sour about it too."

"I know that, Reese, I don't blame you..."

"But you did, Sarah," Reese interrupted, "I came back, but you'd already shut me out."

"I was angry. I wanted to shut you out..." said Sonner, and then she realized this was probably the first time she'd admitted that to Reese or herself. She took a breath, realizing that both of their voices were growing louder and starting to draw interested glances from others in the room. She lowered her voice and continued, "...and I couldn't trust that you wouldn't change your mind again. I never wanted to be the reason you gave up on Earth Fleet, Reese. You'd resent me for that. You had to want it for yourself."

Reese ran a hand through his hair and blew out a sigh. "Look at us. Three hundred years after the end of the world, and we're still at each other's throats like..."

"Like an old married couple?" Sonner suggested, completing his sentence.

"Yeah, just like that," said Reese, smiling again. "Hell, none of it matters now, Sarah, but for what it's worth, I'm sorry."

Sarah reached across the table and took Reese's hands again. "It does matter, Reese," she said squeezing his palms gently. "How we feel, the mistakes we make and what we do about them – that's what makes us human. We have to do everything we can to make sure that survives; to make sure humanity survives." Then she looked down at the table again and added, timidly, "But for what it's worth, I'm sorry too."

Sonner couldn't see them because she was still looking down at the off-white table top, but Reese's eyes grew wide. In their five years together, Sonner had rarely apologized for anything, at least not in words. He knew how hard it would have been for her to do so then. Their brief, contemplative silence made them suddenly aware of the now dozens of pairs of eyes all watching them. It was like being under a spotlight, making them feel hot and uncomfortable. They both sat back, drawing their hands away and onto their laps and trying hard to look normal.

"So, what is it you need me to do, Sarah," said

Reese, after most of the eyes had eventually peeled away. "What's this amazing plan to flip the odds in our favor?"

"Collins has your crew on quick reaction alert, right?" said Sonner, feeling more comfortable and confident now that they'd moved beyond the personal stuff. But, she also felt like a heavy load had been lifted. She was glad that circumstances had forced her to speak to Reese, because if she was honest with herself, she knew she wouldn't have done so otherwise.

"Yeah, that's why we're sitting in here, drinking coffee and not something stronger," said Reese, then he grimaced down at the cup in front of him, "though I'd hesitate to call this sludge coffee..." Sonner smiled. A love of coffee was one of the things they shared. After leaving Earth Fleet, they had planned to start a boutique coffee shop together, roasting the beans in-house and playing around with different brewing techniques. "Not that it would matter if we were half-cooked, anyway, because I don't know how quickly any of us can react when it means piloting out through that damn tunnel."

"For what I need you to do, you'll already be outside this lava tube," said Sonner.

"Go on, I'm listening..."

"When the fleet departs for the attack on Earth, the Hedalt Corvette will break away," continued

Sonner, keeping her voice low so that nearby tables couldn't overhear, "Collins will probably order it to be pursued and destroyed. I need you to stick close to it and get in the way."

"Get in the way..." Reese repeated, as if the words were the most insane that Sonner had ever spoken to him.

"Yes, get in the way," Sonner reiterated, ignoring Reese's growing discomfort. "I need you to make sure no other ship can get a shot off without risk of hitting you. Collins will order you to break off so one of the other ships can attack, but whatever you do, don't. Tell Collins you're having weapons difficulties, or comms problems; whatever, I don't care. Just give that Corvette time to jump."

Sonner had never seen Reese look as scared or as flabbergasted as he did right in that moment. He anxiously checked the other tables around him, but the room had gone back to minding their own business and no-one was paying attention to their exchange anymore. Reese swallowed hard and leant in towards Sonner.

"Are you out of your damn mind?" he asked, managing to control his voice and maintain a mostly neutral expression, despite feeling like he needed to jump up and yell at her. "Why in the hell would I do that?"

"Because the Hedalt already have an armada at

Earth that is at least twice the strength we have, maybe more," said Sonner now with ice-cold seriousness, "and once they detect our fleet jumping the threads, they'll only send more. We have no chance in a straight up firefight, Reese. No chance at all."

"But, how do you know that?" said Reese, stress leaking into his voice and expression.

"Taylor has the ability to hook into the CoreNet and travel inside the Fabric," Sonner continued. "He's seen the fleet at Earth, but Collins won't listen to him. He thinks he's a Hedalt spy or something."

"Well, have you considered that he might be, Sarah?" asked Reese. The tone of his voice was almost accusatory. "He used to be one of their programmed automaton killers for crying out loud!" Reese had raised his voice again and was starting to draw attention back to their table.

Sonner's face remained glacially calm and she waited until the renewed interest had faded before speaking. "I trust Taylor Ray with my life, Reese. Besides you, there's no-one I trust more, living or in the past. He's one of us. None of us would be here if it weren't for him."

Reese rubbed his face and let out another deep sigh. "Not everyone thinks so, Sarah," he said, lowering his voice again. "Collins hasn't been shy about voicing his reservations, and people are listening. A lot of the crews are uncomfortable having them around. It doesn't help that his ship has been showing them up in combat drills for the last week or so."

"Collins is an asshole," Sonner snapped back, briefly losing her iron grip over her emotions, "I wouldn't trust him to lead me through a doorway, never mind into a battle for the fate of humanity."

"Jeez, Sarah, don't make it sound so melodramatic..."

"Wake up, Reese," Sarah snapped again, "that's not being dramatic! That's *exactly* what this is all about. Collins is going to get us all killed, except this time there is no Contingency. Dead means dead, Reese. Dead means the end of the human race."

Sonner's last speech had the sobering effect of a bucket of ice water being tipped over Reese's head and the blood suddenly rushed from his face. He quickly checked that no-one was looking and then shook his head, knowing he would regret what he was about to do.

"Before I agree to help your robot friends get away – which is treason, by the way – you have to tell me why, Sarah. What can one ship do against the entire Hedalt armada?"

"Are you sure you want to know?" asked Sonner, cocking her head to the side. "Plausible deniability, and all that?

"If I'm going to stick my neck out, and risk the lives of my crew, I need to know why."

"You could tell Collins that you did it for your ex-wife, whom you've never stopped loving..." said Sonner, with a wry smirk.

"I thought you said *plausible* deniability," Reese answered, with a matching smirk.

Sonner scowled, "Ouch..." but then she smiled. "Okay, if you really want to know, Taylor has a plan to disable every simulant in the galaxy. There's a single space station that controls them all, and he's going to blow it up."

From his reaction, this was clearly not an answer that Reese had anticipated, but he seemed buoyed by it. "But that would cripple their ships," he said, suddenly realizing how profound an advantage that would give them. "Your robot friend can really do that?"

"It's no less crazy than the stunts that crew has already pulled off," said Sonner, "so, yes, I think he can. Providing, of course, his ship is given time to jump away."

"I'll make sure they get away, Sarah, you have my word on that," said Reese, now oozing confidence. Then he added, "On one condition."

Sonner frowned, "What?"

"If we win this thing, and we both make it through alive, we give 'us' a second chance."

Sonner laughed and brushed her hair from her

eyes, "And you say *I'm* out of my damn mind!"

"I mean it, Sarah," said Reese. Now he was the one talking with a cold seriousness. "A second chance for Earth, a second chance for us. It's only fair. What do you say?"

"Okay, Captain Reese Turner," said Sonner, coyly, "If we achieve the impossible and actually pull this off, then maybe there's hope for impossible relationships too."

Reese smiled, and then blithely added, "You're talking about me and you, not you and Taylor Ray, right?"

Sonner laughed and shook her head, "You're an idiot, Reese." But then they took each other's hands again and smiled.

THIRTEEN

Due to its unique, many-faceted connection to the Fabric, Vice Provost Adra was able to jump her new Destroyer from the Nexus to the star system where the anomaly originated in two hops. From any other location in the galaxy, it would have required many times that number, given the Destroyer's limited jump capabilities.

The first jump was excruciatingly painful, even compared to the agony that Adra had experienced while double-jumping the frigate. Fortunately, her period of recovery on the Hedalt home world had given her the strength to endure it. Even so, as they emerged from the second jump, Adra had to grab hold of the pedestal on which her console screen was mounted in order to stave off the dizziness and blinding pain that tore through her head and neck. Quickly glancing across to Vika at the front of the compact bridge, Adra noted that her Adjutant had done the same. Nonetheless, her ability to endure the savage mental and physical strains of super-luminal travel was as impressive as her fighting skills had been back on the Nexus.

"Jump complete, Vice Provost," said Vika with only a few seconds delay from the point at which they had emerged out of the Fabric. Adra knew that she would be feeling the same as she did, or worse, but she hid it perfectly from her voice.

Though they had not spoken of their fight since it had happened, Adra sensed that Vika had already analyzed why she lost. In short, Adra had gotten under her skin, drawing destabilizing emotions to the fore; emotions she was now burying deep down. Adra knew this would only serve to make her stronger and more dangerous. Once they had destroyed the human base, and Vika brought her challenge again, she knew that the second fight would be the hardest of her life.

"Charge weapons and set a course for the second moon of the fourth planet," ordered Adra, as a medical drone flitted out from its perch and continued to patch up the damage to Adra's face, head and neck. Though the worst of their injuries had been repaired at the advanced medical facility on the Nexus, Adra did not want to wait any longer than was necessary to get underway; as such, work to heal them continued as they travelled. Vika was being attended to by a similar device, and both had removed their black coats and armored jackets to allow the drones to work unobstructed, revealing the extensive nature of the injuries they had sustained. Injuries that would have been fatal to the average human.

"Yes, Vice Provost," Vika replied dutifully, but Adra could see from her small console screen that Vika had already programmed the route and begun charging the weapons. She then placed her hand on the shoulder of the pilot simulant to execute the command, displaying the same ceremonial precision as she had done while executing all of Adra's commands.

They traveled the distance from their jump entry point to the second moon in silence, save for the low thrum of the ship's engines and occasional chaotically-melodic bleep from the various consoles and stations on the bridge. Vika issued a command to the pilot simulant to enter a high orbit, and then began working at her console, still without a word to Adra. But Adra was too consumed with her own work to notice or care. From reviewing the data on the rogue Hunter Corvette's attack on the reclamation facility, Adra had learned that the two human transport ships had departed from a base concealed inside a lava tube on the planet. As such, she had been focusing sensor scans on the moon, looking for former volcanic regions and cave formations, but she had yet to find anything of significance.

"Vice Provost, I believe I may have found something of interest," said Vika after an hour had passed, during which time Adra had discovered nothing of value. Vika enhanced a location on the moon's surface on the viewport, but Adra could only see a tall cluster of rocks. Then Vika highlighted a section of the rock cluster and overlaid a metallurgical scan, which picked up a regular shape hidden within the rocks, something that was unlikely to be naturally occurring. "It is possibly a communications mast or sensor tower," Vika added.

"Scan for nearby cave structures," said Adra, turning from the viewport back to her own console screen.

"The composition of the volcanic rock in this region is preventing our scans from penetrating the surface," Vika commented, "but I have found a cave opening, not far from the location of the metal structure." Vika threw the image up on the viewport and they both studied it with sharp, attentive eyes.

"That is it," said Adra, certain they had found the entrance to the human base, "Take us to the mouth of the cave, I want to see if our scans can penetrate through the tunnel."

"Yes, Vice Provost," said Vika, placing a hand on the pilot simulant's shoulder, prompting it to begin maneuvering the dragonfly-like Destroyer over to the narrow cave.

Adra focused her scans into the throat of the tunnel, rapidly assessing the data as it appeared on her console. "There are sections of the inner cave wall that have been damaged recently," said Adra out loud, though she was as much talking to herself as to Vika, "and there are traces of metals in the gouged sections." She smiled and then sneered, "The human pilots clearly lack the skill to navigate this tunnel."

Suddenly, Vika's station sounded an alert, and she switched to review it with lightning reflexes. "There is a power signature inside the tunnel," Vika announced, as new data continued to flood onto her screen, "It's getting stronger... It's a ship!" Without waiting for Adra's order, she grabbed the pilot's simulant's shoulder and cried, "Take evasive action, now!" but it was already too late. As the nose of a Nimrod-class cruiser emerged from the shadows, its forward cannons flashed.

Vika's decisive action meant they narrowly avoided a crippling strike to the command section, which would have instantly killed Adra and Vika too. Instead the cannon shells pummeled into ventral armor as the Destroyer lifted away from the cave, smashing open the hull and exposing the aft section to the thin atmosphere of the moon. Alarms erupted all over the bridge as the force of the impact sent Adra careening off the low command platform and into the side wall of the bridge. Vika had managed to stay standing, clasped to the back of the pilot's chair like a limpet. As soon as the ship leveled off, Vika threw the pilot simulant from its chair and dropped down in its place. Adra scrambled back to the command platform, blood leaking from a gash to the top of her head, and grabbed the command pedestal, almost tearing it from its mounting.

"Fire aft turrets!" she yelled, turning to where the simulant at the tactical console should have been positioned. Instead she saw its broken and burned body twitching on the deck in front of the charred remains of the station. She roared with frustration and switched her console to the tactical layout, before quickly laying down a spread of plasma fire directly aft. She had no idea if the Nimrod was pursuing, but she wanted it to know they weren't out of the fight yet.

"Three Nimrod-class cruisers have emerged from the cave mouth!" Vika cried, her eyes flicking between the main viewport and the pilot's console, which showed three red chevrons closing fast. The ship shuddered again as smaller turret rounds fired from the lead Nimrod snaked across their hull.

"Can we outrun them?" Adra yelled, as she locked onto one of the trailing Nimrods and fired the port turrets, watching the narrow beams of plasma burrow into the Earth Fleet vessel. It fell back, but didn't break off. Then they were rocked again. Consoles blew out, with the pilot simulant taking the brunt of the energy, blasting its torso into chunks of melted synthetics and metal. Gas vented from cracked conduits and electrical fires started to grow out of control. Flames engulfed the disabled simulant body, melting the synthetic skin on its face and turning it into a ghoulish caricature of itself.

"Negative!" Vika cried back, "Main engines are damaged. It is impossible to escape!"

"Then take us low!" shouted Adra, "Use the terrain to evade them – we must not fall!"

Vika turned the Destroyer back towards the craggy surface of the moon as more cannon and turret rounds raced past them and out towards space. Ahead was a dense mountainous region with a deep ravine cutting between the sheer cliff faces, and Vika urged the damaged Destroyer towards it, pushing as much power into the engines and thrusters as she could pull together. In space the damaged engines lacked the straight line thrust to break away from the Nimrods, but weaving through the moon's thin atmosphere she had a chance. It would come down to her piloting skills versus theirs. Skill versus skill alone.

Adra continued to fire bursts from the aft turrets, forcing the Nimrods to jink and correct their courses to avoid being hit, and with each evasive maneuver, the Earth Fleet ships lost ground to the Destroyer. By chance one of the trailing Nimrods turned into a volley of plasma shards, heavily damaging its aft quarter and forcing it to fall back and disengage from the pursuit, just as Vika swooped into the deep ravine. Flames now began to lick at the base of Adra's boots, but it did not break her laser-like focus. She continued to fire back at the Nimrods, while hastily directing repair drones to patch up the critical systems.

Cannon rounds flashed past and smashed into the cliff face ahead of them, but Vika maneuvered around the toppling rocks, evading the larger hunks. On the pilot's console, she saw one of the two remaining Nimrods peel off from the pursuit. *Cowards!* she cried out in her mind as she pressed the Destroyer deeper into the mountains. Ahead, she could see the ravine fork into three, with one of the paths disappearing beneath high overhangs. It was a perilous route to take, even in a small ship such as the Destroyer, but she was confident she could make it through. Then she had an idea; if she could collapse the overhangs at the moment they passed though, the remaining Nimrod would have no choice but to withdraw or risk being pummeled or even buried under the rock fall.

"Fire dorsal turrets on my command!" Vika shouted. On any other occasion, an adjutant issuing a command to a vice provost would have been unthinkable, but their relationship had transcended Warfare Command protocol long ago. Besides, Adra would not attack Vika while she needed her; and right now, she needed her.

Adra was too preoccupied to respond to Vika's insolence, though in truth she found she was not provoked by it either. By joining her in disobeying Kagan's directives, Vika was no more an officer of Warfare Command than she was. They were both renegades now, and though their causes were different – Adra's to destroy humanity and Vika's to take revenge for her brother's death – their current common purpose of staying alive was all that was needed to maintain the delicate truce.

"Fire!" shouted Vika, as the Destroyer soared under the high rocky overhangs. On cue, Adra released shards of plasma from the two dorsal turrets mounted just inside the Destroyer's wings, collapsing the roof of the ravine behind them. Vika then swung the Destroyer down the narrowest of the three forks, but the damaged thrusters lacked the power to overcome the ship's momentum and they collided with the rock face. Alarms rang out again as more consoles and conduits exploded, taking the bridge lighting out with it, leaving only the glow from the main viewport for illumination. Vika shunted all the power she could into the thrusters and dragged the ship off the rocks. Behind them the final Nimrod had been unable to pursue, and was instead gaining altitude, attempting to spot them from above, like a hawk hunting prey.

Vika wrestled the Destroyer away from the cliff face and tucked it underneath a deep overhang, concealing it from view. Engaging the landing struts she then dropped the ship down hard onto the uneven rock and quickly powered down the engines to reduce their energy signature. She climbed out of the pilot's seat and turned to Adra, "We must shut down the weapons and all non-essential systems!" she called over, but Adra was already in the process of powering everything else down, bar essential life support to the bridge only.

"We know the rocks on this moon are an effective shield against sensors," Vika added, as power bled out of the ship's remaining functional systems, accompanied by a low, descending hum. "I do not believe the Earth vessel will be able to detect us."

"We must accelerate repairs to the ship," said Adra, reaching down to extinguish the flames that had begun to creep up her boots. "They will assume we communicated their location to Warfare Command, and they will soon abandon their base to launch for Earth. We must collapse this lava tube and entomb them here forever."

Vika had been checking the scale of the damage on her console while Adra was putting out her personal fires. "The damage is extensive. It includes external sensors and our link to the CoreNet. It will be many hours before we are capable of what you suggest. Kagan will have traced our jump by now. He will be coming."

"Kagan will not have this victory!" Adra growled as she redistributed the repair drones to work on the essential systems that would allow them to get under way in the shortest possible time. "The humans are mine to destroy!" Repair drones began to circle around the bridge, frantically extinguishing fires and darting from section to section, patching up the vital systems. Looking up from her console, Adra turned to Vika and snarled, "Activate the reserve simulants. Direct them to assist with repairs. Now!"

Vika could hear the strain in Adra's voice and recognized the flash of madness in her eyes. It was a look she had once seen staring back in her own reflection, in the moments after she had learned of her brother's death. Vika knew only too well the dangers of letting emotions cloud her judgment. Emotion had caused her to intervene in Adra's tribunal in the naive hope it would allow her to take personal revenge for Lux. That misjudgment had caused the loss of her position and status. She had allowed Adra to rile her during their fight; it had clouded her judgment and handed the Vice Provost the victory. She had given her word that she would follow Adra's commands until she had defeated the humans, or no prospect of that remained, but it was clear to her now that they would play no further role in the war to come. She considered issuing her challenge then and there, on the smashed and smoke-filled bridge, while Adra was distracted and consumed with anger. But it would do no good to kill her now, not while their broken ship lay stranded with the enemy circling above, looking for an opportunity to finish them off. But the time would soon come when Adra would have to accept defeat and failure. And then, when Adra was at her lowest ebb, she would finally settle her debt.

Vika bowed her head and simply replied, "Yes, Vice Provost."

FOURTEEN

Commander Sarah Sonner burst through the ready room doors and ran into the hangar bay just as the rear ramp of the last Nimrod thumped into the metal decking. The other two Nimrods were already on-station beside it, with crews working to patch up the damage sustained from the battle with the Hedalt warship. Sonner reached the Nimrod just as Captain Reese Turner stepped down onto the deck.

Sonner caught Reese by the shoulders, "Are you okay?" she asked, quickly checking him over.

"I'm fine, Commander," said Reese, sticking to character since the ship was already being overrun by repair crews. Reese's other three crew members then began to make their way down the ramp and Sonner quickly pulled her hands away, pressing them to the small of her back instead.

"Did you destroy the enemy ship, Captain?" she asked, quickly switching back to her pricklier 'commander' persona as the crew approached.

"I don't know for sure," Reese admitted. "We hit that sucker pretty hard, but it dove into a deep series of ravines running through the mountain range, maybe a hundred clicks north, and then we lost contact."

"Damn it, then we have to assume it's still out there. Either way, this base has been exposed." Sonner met the eyes of Reese's crew members, who had all hung back while they talked, wary of a repeat performance from the ready room, then looked back at Reese. "Stay alert, we may need to get out of here in a hurry."

Suddenly klaxons began to blare out in the hangar bay and the evacuation signal lights pulsed on and off. A crackly voice came over the intercom, "All hands, evacuate the base immediately. All ships are to immediately jump to rally point alpha. Repeat... evacuate the base, all ships are to immediately jump to rally point alpha." Reese and Sonner stared around the hangar bay as panicked crews hustled onto the deck and began racing towards their ships.

"Looks like you spoke too soon..." said Reese, and then he turned to his crew. "Shore leave is over folks, get back on board and get the ship prepped. I'll be back in ten." They all nodded frantically, eyes wide with fright, and ran back on-board.

"I need to get to the command center and find out what the hell is going on," said Sonner, setting off at a jog.

Reese followed, "I'll come with you," he called out, "I want to know what we're facing too."

Streams of flight and engineering teams raced past them in the other direction until they reached the central command and control center. She saw Taylor standing behind one of the few remaining crew members that was still on-station and ran over to him.

"What is it?" Sonner blurted out so suddenly that she made Taylor recoil.

"Damn it, Sarah, you scared the life out of me," Taylor complained, and then he saw that Sonner wasn't alone. "Oh, sorry, I didn't know there was someone with you."

"Don't sweat it," said Reese, extending a hand, which Taylor accepted, "Captain Reese Turner. I've heard a lot about you."

"You have?" said Taylor, and then Reese let out a yelp as Taylor inadvertently added too much pressure to his grip. "Sorry about that," said Taylor hastily releasing his hold, "I literally don't know my own strength."

Reese shook the pain away, but he was smiling,

"I guess being a simulant has some benefits, huh?"

"Well, it beats being dead," said Taylor, "and it means I clean up in arm wrestling contests."

The two men laughed and Sonner shook her head, "You two finished? Good. Now, what are we dealing with?"

Taylor turned back to the console screen as a recording of the evacuation message played out over the speakers again, "Five more ships just jumped in, and they're nearly on top of us. I'd say these ones already knew where to look. Most likely, they picked up the residual ion trails from the four that were high-burning it around the moon earlier."

"Yeah, that was me," said Reese, holding his hands up. But then he frowned, "Just five more ships, though? That doesn't sound so urgent."

"Maybe not, but we intercepted a signal from the lead vessel," said Taylor. "This is just the welcoming party; reinforcements are on the way." Taylor then leaned across the console and brought up the long-range scan analysis of the approaching squadron. "And they're not just any five ships, either. Four of them are War Frigates – the Commander and I know all about those – but the fifth is something new."

Reese let out a long, low whistle. "That thing is freakin' huge!"

"Thanks for that expert assessment, Captain,"

said Sonner, snarkily, as she studied the data, "It's a capital ship of some kind, maybe even a carrier."

"I don't know what it is, but I've seen it before, during one of the first times I entered the Fabric," said Taylor. If he was still human, his body would have felt a shiver as he recalled the memory. "It was at Earth, so it's a fair call to suggest it will be on the front line when we attack."

"Not if we take it out here," said Reese, smarting a little from Sonner's jab. "We have a hundred ships. We could take out these five before the cavalry arrives, and while we still have the advantage. It would mean we then don't have to contend with them at Earth."

"That's what I'd do," agreed Taylor, "but our esteemed Colonel has other ideas."

Sonner growled, which was all she could do to stop from screaming at the top of her lungs, "Damn that fool! Where is he now?"

"He's on Nimrod Command", said Taylor, "And by the way, he asked me to tell you – not very politely I may add – to get on-board 'posthaste' if I saw you first."

"Posthaste?" said Reese. "Who the hell talks like that?"

"I'll see if I can shake some sense into him," said Sonner, though she didn't sound hopeful. "For now, get to your ships and out of this lava tube, before those warships turn it into a tomb." Then she slapped the crewman who was working at the console on the shoulder, "You too, mister. Evacuate the command and control room."

The crewman shot out of his seat as if it had been electrocuted and raced towards the corridor leading to the hangar deck, closely followed by the three other remaining control room staff. Reese and Taylor laughed.

"It looks like your special mission won't be necessary after all, Reese," said Sonner, raising her eyebrows at him, "I'll see you at rally point alpha." Then she turned to Taylor and sighed, "I'm no good at goodbyes, Captain..."

"That's not been my experience..." Reese cut in, getting his own back for Sonner's earlier snide remark, but the look he got in return could have melted lead.

"As I was saying..." Sonner said, turning her back to Reese, but then Taylor held up his hands to stop her.

"No goodbyes, Commander," said Taylor, "they're too final. Let's just say, 'until next time', okay?"

Sonner nodded and smiled, "Good luck Taylor. Until next time..." then she turned back to Reese. "I'll see you at rally point alpha, okay?"

"Not if I see you first, Commander." He replied, then he smoothed the loose strands of her hair back and gently kissed her on the forehead. "Give the Colonel hell."

"I will..." Sonner answered, and set off back towards the hangar deck. She had only taken a few paces, before she stopped and again met Taylor's silver simulant eyes. "Make sure you find her Taylor," she said. It was phrased as an order, but spoken with deep affection. "Make sure you put your crew back together."

Taylor smiled and threw up a lazy salute, "Aye, aye, Commander Sarah Sonner."

Taylor and Reese remained and watched Sonner as she hurried off along the corridor to the hangar deck, steeling herself for yet another confrontation with Colonel Collins. Then once they were alone, Reese turned back to Taylor and smiled again.

"You know, it takes a lot to get in Sarah's good graces, take it from someone who knows."

Taylor had been wondering why Reese had accompanied Sonner, right up to the point where he kissed her on the head, and then the penny had dropped. "You're her ex-husband, right?" Reese smiled and nodded.

"She asked you to be our blocker, didn't she?" Taylor continued, piecing it all together. "And you agreed?"

"Let's just say she made a pretty compelling argument," Reese answered, slightly evasively. "The truth is, Captain, I have no idea if you're a robot, or a Hedalt spy like Collins says, or if you're just as human as the rest of us. But if what you say you saw at Earth is true, I do know that we don't have a hope in hell of beating the Hedalt armada. So anything you can do to even the odds has to be worth a shot."

"Well, I appreciate your honesty, Captain," said Taylor.

"Call me Reese."

"Okay, Reese." He shrugged, "To level with you, I don't really know what I am either. But I'm certainly no spy."

"I believe you," said Reese, slapping him on the shoulder. "Besides, Sarah trusts you and believes in you. I'd say she's never trusted or believed in anyone more in her entire life, except for perhaps one other."

"So what went wrong?"

Reese took a deep breath and rubbed his chin, "I wasn't ready to commit. I chickened out. And then when I came to my senses... well, it was already too late."

"It's never too late," said Taylor firmly, "not until it's over."

Reese smiled and half-nodded, half-shrugged, "I hope you're right." Then he straightened up, "So, can you do this thing, whatever this thing is that you're planning to do?"

"Yes, I believe I can," said Taylor, confidently.

"Providing I can get out of this base and jump away without either Colonel Collins or that Hedalt squadron blowing my ship to pieces."

"Don't sweat it, Captain Taylor Ray," replied Reese, cheerfully, "you've got yourself a blocker."

FIFTEEN

Taylor ran on to the bridge of the Contingency One and spotted Casey and Blake already at their stations. He dropped down in the command chair and glanced towards the mission ops station, which was empty. At his sister's insistence, James had been reassigned to Nimrod Command, the designated command ship where Colonel Collins and Commander Sonner would direct the battle for Earth.

"It will be strange without James at mission ops," said Casey, spinning around and throwing up a lazy salute to Taylor. "I was getting used to having him around."

Then the console in Taylor's chair bleeped to notify him of an incoming communication from Nimrod Command. "Speak of the devil..." said

Taylor, routing the message through to the bridge audio system.

"Nimrod Fleet, this is Nimrod Command," said the slightly wobbly voice of James Sonner, "All ships stand by for hangar deck decompression. Once complete, all vessels are to exit the base in squadron order, smartly. Nimrod Command, out."

Blake leant over the back of his chair with a puzzled look on his face. "Are we s'posed to be in one of these squadrons?"

Taylor smiled, "We're a squadron of one, and we go last. Apparently, Collins considers us less important that the 'human' ships."

Blake growled, "I swear if the two Sonners weren't on Nimrod Command, I'd blow that ship to hell right now."

"I know how you feel," sighed Taylor, "but it actually plays to our advantage. Hopefully, by the time we get out, half of the fleet will have already jumped away. It should make it easier to sneak off unnoticed."

The audio link to Nimrod Command clicked on and James Sonner's voice again came through over the speakers. "Hangar bay decompression in five... four... three... two... one..."

Taylor and the others watched as micro-explosions rippled across the entire front wall of the hangar bay, like dominoes falling in line. Each detonation blasted away one of the bolts fixing the wall in place, until there were none left. Then, as the hangar rapidly decompressed, the wall was pushed outwards, crashing through the open airlock and out into the gloom of the lava tube.

"Won't it take too long for a hundred ships to squeeze through that tunnel, one at a time?" said Blake, as the first squadron of Nimrods powered out of the hangar.

"It would, but that's not the plan," replied Taylor. "This base is burned. We can't come back while the threat from the Hedalt armada remains, so the lead Nimrod squadron is going to collapse the cave ceiling at the far end."

Blake's console bleeped and he turned to check it. "Wow, those guys move fast..." he commented.

"What do you mean?" asked Taylor, pushing out of his seat and moving to Blake's side. "There's no way they can already be in position."

"Well, the cave's collapsin' now, so if it ain't them, then who?"

Taylor felt his senses heighten, "Put the area on the viewport," he ordered, and then quickly returned to his chair. Blake tapped the commands into his console and the viewport switched to a magnified section of the cave ceiling, several kilometers across the other side of the lava tube. Just as Blake had said, it was collapsing, raining huge chunks of volcanic rock onto the abandoned residential blocks that occupied the far side of the base. But there were no Nimrods in sight.

Taylor punched up an audio link to Nimrod Command using the console in his chair, "Commander, are you seeing this too?"

"We see it, Captain," said the voice of Sarah Sonner. She sounded composed, but still rushed through the sentence. "Stand by for plan B."

"What's plan B?" asked Taylor, wondering if he'd somehow missed that part of the briefing for the base evacuation plan.

"I'll tell you when we have one, Sonner out..."

The communications link went dead. Casey and Blake exchanged concerned glances and then both turned to Taylor, but the focus on him was short-lived as alerts suddenly rang out from all stations. They all peered back up at the viewport as a massive section of the ceiling fell down, opening up a hole several hundred meters in diameter. But visible through the opening was more than just the hazy atmosphere of the moon; there was also the outline of a ship many times larger than anything they'd encountered before. Silhouetted against the glow of the system's star, the goliath ship hung above them like a giant manta ray, silent and still. Then its underbelly suddenly lit up as dozens of shards of purple plasma flashed into the lava tube, directly towards the base.

"Casey, get us out of here, I don't care how!" Taylor cried, as plasma shards hammered into the surrounding structures of the Contingency base.

"Aye, aye, Captain Taylor Ray!" replied Casey, pulling the pilot's viewport into position. Then she glanced at Blake, "Hey, do you think you can make me a little door?"

"Already on it, Casey," said Blake, firing the forward cannons and blasting a chunk out of the stone wall alongside the already open section.

The hole was barely larger than the profile of the compact Corvette, but Casey surged the ship forward, adjusting the angle and axis of the vessel with surgical precision, and managed to squeeze through and out into the lava tube ahead of the remaining Nimrod squadrons.

"Jeez, Casey, that was close!" cried Blake, gripping his chair as if he was on a rollercoaster that was about to dip down.

Casey drew back from the pilot's viewport and winked at him, "Quit complaining; you could have made the hole a little bigger..."

A fleet-wide broadcast interrupted any further banter. It was from Nimrod Command and Taylor put it on speakers.

"Nimrod squadrons Alpha One and Alpha Two, concentrate fire on the opening in the cave ceiling. We need to crack it wider so the fleet can slip through. Nimrod Squadrons Beta One, Beta Two, engage that ship and push it back. All other Squadrons, just get the hell out of this cave and jump to the rendezvous point!"

"She don't need to tell me twice!" said Blake, as a plasma shard as thick as a tree trunk flashed past, obliterating one of the Nimrods that had just exited the hangar bay. Casey took evasive action, but they had all seen how devasting a single shot from the capital ship had been.

"Casey, I'd really appreciate it if you could steer clear of that ship's big guns."

"It's on my to-do list, Cap!" Casey called back, weaving between one of the fleeing Nimrod squadrons to race ahead of it.

At the far end of the lava tube Taylor could see the opening begin to widen further as the lead Nimrod squadrons pummeled cannon rounds into the rock. But the dust hadn't even settled before the imposing sight of a War Frigate filled the gap. "Damn it, we're like rabbits trapped in a warren down here," said Taylor, "Casey, can you punch us through?"

"Shouldn't we help the fleet, Cap?" shouted Casey, as she weaved the Contingency One around another of the slower-moving Nimrods. Two more ships were hit ahead of them and ignited into fiery hunks, causing Casey to take sudden evasive action. "Hang on!" she cried as she banked hard right and spun between exploding sections of broken hull. Fragments of metal and debris bounced off their armor like flaming meteorites.

"On second thoughts, scratch that idea, Cap. If we hang around in here for much longer, we'll be pulverized!"

"Just pick an opening and hit it, Casey!" shouted Taylor, "If we don't get out, it doesn't matter how many of the Nimrods survive. They only have a chance if we take down the Nexus!"

The console in Taylor's chair bleeped again. It was a tactical alert. *What now?* he thought, wondering what else could go wrong. He scanned the data, but then he wished he hadn't asked. "Hedalt reinforcements have just jumped in," Taylor called out to the others. "Fifty warships... correction, make that seventy ships! Casey, it's time to leave..."

"I'm on it, Cap!" cried Casey as she surged towards the smashed opening in the lava tube. Plasma shards lit up the darkness as she jinked and weaved and spun the ship, using every ounce of her considerable piloting skill and ingenuity to make her course as chaotic as possible to avoid the incoming fire. But she couldn't help noticing that the Hedalt were far more focused on them than the rest of the fleet. "They're not making it easy on us!"

Taylor noted that Nimrod Squadrons Beta One and Beta Two were now directly engaged with the capital ship, but it was like shooting BB pellets at a medieval suit of armor, and three of the ten ships had already been destroyed. *Come on, come on!* Taylor urged as he watched the counter for the number of ships that had escaped slowly creep up. *Twenty... Twenty four... Come on!*

Suddenly the ship was rocked and Taylor grabbed the arm of the chair, putting another dent in it due to his inhuman strength.

"Direct hit!" cried Blake, and then there was a tense pause, "but we're okay... minor damage... the armor soaked up most of it."

Taylor inspected the summarized damage report on his console, "Luckily it was from one of their smaller turrets," he called out. "But if we take a hit like that from the main cannons, we're done for."

"Noted!" shouted Casey, as she dodged another volley of plasma fire. "Hold on to your pants, because I'm going to make my run through the opening in five... four..." But Casey didn't reach three, as the hawk-like outline of another War Frigate appeared above the gap she was aiming for, "Damn it, Cap, that route's a bust too!" she cried out swinging the Contingency One back around and further into the lava tube again, as a savage volley of plasma flashed past their hull.

"Keep looking, Casey," Taylor called back, "Any opening you see, take it!"

The communications system bleeped again, but this time it wasn't a communication from Nimrod

Command, it was from Nimrod Delta One. *Who the hell is this?* Taylor thought as he opened the link.

"Hey, Captain, I thought you could use a hand," came the voice of Captain Reese Turner.

"Reese? What are you doing, get yourself out!" Taylor called back, "Colonel Collins will be too preoccupied with getting the fleet to safety to care about us."

"Sure, though I couldn't help but notice that you're still here, Captain," said Reese. "Collins may let you go, but these big-ass Hedalt ships seem to have taken a particular dislike to you. It's why the rest of the fleet is managing to slip out."

"He's right, Cap," Blake called back, "They're focusin' fire heavily on us. It's like there's a damn bounty on our head or somethin'. We must've hacked 'em off worse than we thought!"

"What do you propose, Captain?" Taylor said into the communicator. He was reluctant to let Reese put his neck on the line for them, but he knew he was right. The Nimrod Fleet had no chance against the Hedalt Armada if they couldn't reach the Nexus and shut down the simulants.

"Just stay tight in my shadow, Captain," Reese said, "and then when you see a patch of starry sky, run like hell!"

The communications link went dead, and Taylor quickly adjusted the image on the main viewport to display Reese's ship in a small window to the side. "Casey, you heard the man..."

"Aye, aye, Captain Taylor Ray," replied Casey. Then she swung the ship around and tucked it in behind Nimrod Delta One, so perfectly that it would have been almost impossible for the Hedalt to distinguish the two ships from their elevated vantage point outside the cave.

"Get ready to shunt as much power as you can scrounge into the ion drives," ordered Taylor, gripping the arms of his chair so tightly they creaked under the pressure, "Then as soon as we're clear, punch it!"

The two ships accelerated towards the opening and Taylor flitted between checking the status of the fleet and peering out at the massive ships blocking their path. "Forty six out, including Nimrod Command!" cried Taylor. *Sarah and James were safe... that was something, at least...* he thought. Then he saw the casualties and winced, "But we've already lost sixteen Nimrods, and more are taking heavy damage!"

Ninety-nine Nimrods attacking the Hedalt armada was a tall order, but they were already down to eighty-three and they hadn't even reached Earth yet. The more he thought about it, the more it was clear that the Nimrod Fleet's mission was a suicide run. They had to escape and reach the Nexus. If they failed, humanity would become extinct.

"Breaching in ten!" shouted Casey, as she pulled out from beneath Reese's ship and accelerated hard to make her run.

The tactical console sounded an angry alert, "That capital ship has spotted us an' locked on, Cap!" cried Blake, "It's gonna fire!"

"Casey, give us more speed!"

"I'm trying, Cap!" Casey called back. "Breaching in five!"

"Too late, they're firin'!"

A shard of plasma the length of their entire ship erupted from the primary cannons on the War Carrier and seared through the lava tube towards them.

"Brace for impact!" Taylor called out, but then out of nowhere Nimrod Delta One blasted in front of them, taking the hit full on. The entire viewport was engulfed in a searing red and orange blaze, forcing even Taylor to shield his simulant eyes. When the image cleared he looked on in horror at what remained of Reese's ship spiraling out of control, crippled and on fire, before it collided with the Hedalt capital ship and exploded in a violent fit of sparks and flames.

"No!" cried Taylor, but it was too late. Nimrod Delta One was gone. Reese was gone. He hammered the arm of the chair, snapping it clean off, and then sprang to his feet, glaring out at the capital ship as it retreated from the opening, burning and damaged, but still functional.

"We're clear!" shouted Casey, as the Contingency One broke out above the moon's surface, covered in burning debris, "Engines to one hundred and ten percent!"

The glow from their ion engines was so bright they could have been mistaken for a comet surging through the cosmos. The retreat of the Hedalt capital ship had allowed the remaining Nimrods to also break through, but in the process five more had fallen to the barrage of plasma fire from the escorting War Frigates. *Seventy-eight ships left...* Taylor said to himself. *Three times that number would barely be enough...*

As the Hedalt capital withdrew further the War Frigates moved into position above the lava tube. In deep space above them the last of the Nimrods blind-jumped away, narrowly avoiding the armada of Hedalt reinforcements closing in behind. Taylor watched on the viewport as the War Frigates hammered volleys of plasma fire into the lava tube, decimating what remained of the Contingency Base. One thing was certain – no matter what happened at Earth, there was no going back now. Not for any of them.

Taylor saw Casey angrily shove the pilot's viewport away, before practically punching the initiator for the jump countdown. For the first time in his memory of Casey Valera, simulant or otherwise, she was not spinning around in her chair. And she was not smiling. Even Casey had her limits, Taylor realized. But he knew it would likely get worse for the Nimrod Fleet, before it got better. A lot worse.

"Jumping in five...

...F o u r

...T h r e e

... T w o

. . . O n e"

SIXTEEN

Vika had been correct about the repairs to the Destroyer taking longer than Adra had anticipated. After two hours they had only just succeeded in restoring the critical systems needed to resume space travel. This included their external sensor array and uplink to the CoreNet, which was being worked on by one of the two reserve simulants that had replaced the units destroyed in the battle.

Adra stepped down off the command platform and pushed the simulant aside so that she could inspect the sensor feed, which was still being populated with data. Vika appeared at her side, uninvited, but Adra did not acknowledge her presence. They may have only spoken to one other when absolutely necessary, but Adra had still observed her closely, noting that the adjutant's skill set also extended to engineering. Without her efforts the repairs would have certainly taken far longer to complete.

"I am reading no vessels still in the vicinity of this moon or the second planet," said Vika, commenting on the updated sensor feed. "But there is significant residual radiation around the cave entrance. I would suggest that there has been a major engagement."

The CoreNet feed synchronized and a Priority One alert took over the console screen. Adra dismissed the alert and continued to review the sensor data. Vika's eyes flicked across to the Vice Provost, who was still ignoring her presence, and then she moved to an adjacent console to review the Priority One. Whether they would respond to it or not – and Vika was under no illusions that Adra would suddenly be gripped by an urgent sense of duty – she wanted to know the contents of the message.

"Priority One message from Warfare Command," Vika said out loud, summarizing the content. "An Earth Fleet armada comprised of seventy-eight Nimrod-class cruisers has been detected. War vessels are being directed to the Sol system to destroy it. We are amongst the vessels requisitioned for the defense."

Adra grabbed the simulant she had brushed

aside and pushed it towards the front of the bridge. "Take us back to the cave entrance," she growled at it, before turning her attention to Vika. "We will not be responding to the Priority One," she said, calmly but firmly.

"Of course not," replied Vika, making no effort to disguise the fact she considered Adra's statement obvious and unnecessary. "However, the message is clear. The human fleet is heading to Earth, where Kagan will crush them and claim victory." Adra stepped away from the console and faced Vika, understanding the hidden meaning behind her statement. "You have failed, Vice Provost Adra. What remains of the human resistance will soon be defeated. It is time you honored your promise to me."

The ship suddenly edged out from underneath the overhang, under the control of the simulant that Adra had shoved towards the pilot's console, and began making its way towards the human base. Adra stepped back onto the command platform, ensuring she did not take her eyes off Vika even for a second, in case she chose to make a move.

"You will get your chance soon enough," said Adra, peering down at Vika from her elevated position, "but not until the humans are dead. Until that time, you are to obey my commands. That was our bargain."

Vika was perplexed by the response. "Their

defeat is inevitable. You cannot believe that their archaic fleet still has a chance?"

"No," said Adra, who now had half an eye on the viewport as they approached the area of the moon where they had found the cave mouth, but now it was clear that a battle had taken place. Carcasses of ships littered the moon's surface, and where there had once been a small cave opening, there was now a huge gaping hole hundreds of meters wide. "Seventy-eight of their ships stand no chance of defeating our armada. But the humans have not hidden in the shadows for three centuries only to commit suicide now. We are missing something."

Vika frowned but then turned to look at the viewport as Adra commanded the pilot simulant to enter the lava tube. The light from the star shone inside like a giant torch beam, illuminating the base that had been built inside and that had remained concealed for centuries. It was an impressive feat of engineering, Vika considered, noting the hulks of other destroyed Nimrods lying on the cave floor. Adra had a point; for a plan so long in the making, it seemed unlikely the humans would throw it all away by attempting a desperate and hopeless assault against a far superior force.

Vika returned to her station and began to review the report of the assault on the human base that was already available via the CoreNet, looking for anything that seemed unusual or out of place.

Meanwhile, the Destroyer steadily circled inside the lava tube, as if it were an archaeology ship surveying an ancient tomb. It did not take long for Vika to find something that stood out as unusual.

"According to the battle records, after High Provost Kagan's War Carrier was damaged, a fleet of seventy-eight Nimrods jumped away, along with three support vessels," said Vika. "But there was also a single Corvette-class cruiser among the ships listed. However, it is unclear whether it jumped with the rest of the human fleet."

"The rogue Hunter Corvette," agreed Adra, confirming Vika's statement on her own console. "Kagan was trying to destroy it, but he allowed it to escape." Adra could almost taste the bitterness and resentment in her voice, and focused hard to keep her emotions in check.

"It must also have jumped to Earth," suggested Vika. "Kagan already sent squadrons to destroy the human bases in the asteroid belt and on the planet where the reclamation facility is based. And I do not believe the simulant would risk another incursion into the Fabric." Then her mind suddenly returned to the moment on the Nexus when she had been looking at the prototype Satomi Rose simulant and had felt a strange sensation, like an electrical charge. "Unless..." she said, thinking out loud.

The word intrigued Adra and she moved

alongside Vika as the adjutant brought up the records of the signal anomaly that Adra had traced back to their current location from the Nexus. In her haste and eagerness to reach the human base, Adra had not completed the full signal trace. Vika worked the console, noticing that Adra was watching intently at her side. Vika discovered that Adra had only focused on decoding the origin of the signal anomaly, and had not calculated its full route through the Fabric, including its precise destination. Vika completed the calculations and arrived at the result. Adra saw it on Vika's console at the same time and their eyes met.

"The Nexus?" said Adra. She could only think of one reason why the rogue simulant would travel to the Nexus, but it sounded absurd. She said it anyway, and the notion sounded even more preposterous spoken out loud, "They mean to destroy the Nexus?"

"It is a fortress," commented Vika, though her tone was not derisory, since she had arrived at the same conclusion. "They would be destroyed before they even came close to it."

"Yet it is the only way Earth Fleet would ever stand a chance against our forces," said Adra. "That they are even aware of its existence suggests it plays a role in their plan."

Vika frowned, still struggling to believe such a feat could be possible. But, at the same time, she understood the disastrous impact the destruction of the Nexus would have on the entire empire. It would cripple their armada and render most of their outposts and colony planets inoperable. Their empire would collapse, and Earth would fall to the humans.

"They could not possibly hope to destroy it with one ancient ship," said Vika, looking for a way to make sense of their discovery. "There is something else we are not seeing."

Adra looked out at the crippled Earth base on the viewport, raising a clenched fist to her chin, like a frustrated scholar. "But what?" she snarled under her breath, growing more irritated by the second. "What are we missing?"

"Satomi Rose," said Vika. Suddenly it made sense, and the instant she had spoken the name, she had Adra's complete attention. "There is a prototype Satomi Rose simulant inside your lab on the Nexus, along with prototypes of the other three. I discovered it while you were working on the signal trace."

"What of it?" asked Adra, realizing that the rogue Taylor Ray simulant still needed this unit to complete his sentimental reformation of his crew.

"I checked the status display on the units," said Vika. "The Satomi Rose model was viable and was showing neural activity. It is possible it was still connected to the CoreNet."

Adra was indignant, "Why did you not reveal this to me?"

Vika's eyes narrowed, "You were not in a talkative mood, Vice Provost," she snarled back.

Adra backed off. She did not want another confrontation with Vika now, but her information had provided the answer. Not only was the Taylor Ray simulant still obsessed with recovering this last unit, but the Satomi unit may have provided them with a back door into the Nexus. She knew that the Taylor Ray simulant possessed the ability to traverse the Fabric and control elements of the CoreNet, as it had done when taking control of a simulant on her frigate. It was possible it had made contact with this prototype unit, whose neural interfaces remained fully intact, and together they had formulated a plan. But he would not destroy the Nexus with Satomi still inside. It would be his last and only chance to recover her, since every other Satomi Rose unit in the galaxy had already been decommissioned. But, whatever the rogue simulant's plan was, Adra's next destination was clear.

"Set a course for the Nexus, and jump at once," she said, stepping back towards her command platform. Then she paused and turned to face Vika again. "Unless, you would rather us try to kill each other again right now?"

Vika realized her future in Warfare Command

was gone, but she shared Adra's hatred for humankind. She did not want the Empire to crumble and for Earth to be lost to the humans. She looked up at the broken Earth Fleet base, and then back at Adra, before she turned and placed a hand on the shoulder of the pilot simulant and said, "No, Vice Provost. Not yet."

SEVENTEEN

The Contingency One jumped and once again Taylor and his crew fell into the mysterious sub-layer of space called the Fabric. Except that this time, thanks to Taylor having memorized the coordinates that Satomi showed him, they were travelling along one of the unique threads that lead directly to the Nexus.

The jump distance was vast, even by the normal definition of super-luminal travel. The switch in reality from the physical world to that of disembodied, dream-like thought persisted for considerably longer than in normal jumps. But this wasn't the only difference Taylor felt. Instead of only sensing the presence and energy of those directly around him, Taylor could perceive their destination as clearly as if he was connected to the

CoreNet through his specially-adapted bed. He saw the chamber where Satomi had appeared to him, but she wasn't there. This time he saw four stasis pods at the end of a large open hall, each of them containing a simulant. Then he was standing in front of the pods, exactly as if he was inside the Fabric in the deep space corridor. He moved forward and peered through the glass canopy of the first stasis pod. It contained Blake Meade, eyes closed, face and body frozen, like a mannequin. He thought of the original Blake simulant, who had died on the Contingency base, crushed by rock and girders, and the trauma of the memory made Taylor recoil. Yet, curiosity compelled him to look inside the other pods too.

He moved along the row, finding Casey Valera in the second pod and then himself in the third, both appearing exactly the same as Blake. The sight of Casey was even more difficult to handle than his own lifeless reflection staring back at him. Then he glanced across to the fourth pod. He knew who would be inside, but Satomi had been taken from him twice already. He wasn't sure if he could handle losing her for a third time. But he had to know.

Nervously, he looked through the glass of the fourth pod and saw the face of Satomi Rose; motionless, lifeless. He felt the sickening stab of grief, but then suddenly Satomi's silver eyes opened, causing Taylor's mind to jolt, like the sudden shock of tasting an ice-cold drink. He staggered backwards as the door to the pod swung open and Satomi stepped out.

"You're jumping to the Nexus?" asked Satomi.

"Yes," said Taylor, too stunned to answer with anything more elaborate.

"She is too. She knows what you intend to do."

"Who? Adra?"

"Yes, and she wants revenge."

"We'll be ready," said Taylor, determinedly. In many ways he relished the opportunity to face Adra again. She had been like a shadow, constantly following them, creating darkness wherever they managed to light a beacon of hope. Her dark aura had been a constant menace, threatening to consume them whole should they ever remain still for too long. But this time Taylor and his crew would shine so brightly that her shadow would be extinguished, forever.

"You need to land at docking level alpha," said Satomi. Her image was starting to fade, as was the room around them. "I will show you the way."

"But how do we get inside?" asked Taylor with urgency, knowing that the moment they emerged from the jump, he would lose her again.

"The Nexus is expecting you," said Satomi, calmly, "and so am I..."

Suddenly, Taylor was ripped back into reality,

back into the command chair on the bridge of the Contingency One. For a moment, the lights of the bridge were blinding compared to the darkness of the space he had just been in. But once his senses readjusted he was presented with a sight almost as unbelievable as his visions inside the Fabric. In front of them on the viewport was a space station that was so massive it could have almost been mistaken for a moon. Only the metallic glint of its surface and its regular, engineered shape gave it away as artificial.

"Is that the Nexus?" wondered Casey, looking at the object, awestruck.

"I guess it must be," said Taylor, realizing he'd only ever seen part of it from the inside. Then to Blake he said, "What do the tactical sensors make of that thing?"

"If you mean, 'is it dangerous?', then hell yeah, it's dangerous," said Blake, "I'm detecting plasma cannons and turrets and what look like torpedo launch tubes, and a ton of other stuff I don't even want to guess at."

"Are they locking on to us?" asked Taylor.

"Nope, not that I can tell anyway," replied Blake.

"Then it's not dangerous," said Taylor, "at least, not yet."

"You and me have a very different idea of what's dangerous, Cap..." replied Blake, shifting uncomfortably in his seat. "Remind me again why we're doing this?"

"Because it's the right thing to do," said Taylor, and Blake rolled his eyes.

"Aww, come on Blakey, I always had you down as the hero type," teased Casey, shooting a wink at Taylor too.

"I like to think of myself as more the 'I like livin'' type," grumbled Blake.

"What about other Hedalt ships?" said Taylor, ignoring Blake's mutterings.

"Negative, there's just us an' that thing out there," said Blake. "Likely, they've sent their warships to Earth. But honestly, it's not like it needs protection. It has enough firepower to take out an armada on its own."

"Well, there's only one way to find out if it's hostile," said Taylor, "Casey, take us to docking level alpha."

"I'd love to, Cap," said Casey, but then she spun her chair around to face him and added, "any idea where that might be?"

Taylor laughed, "Good point... No, I have absolutely no idea!" Then he thought back to what Satomi had told him. "Satomi just told me that the Nexus was expecting us."

"Satomi?" said Blake, eyeing Taylor with suspicion. "When the hell didya talk to her?"

Taylor rubbed his chin, realizing he hadn't

explained that part, "I sort of spoke to her during the jump over here."

"Right..." said Blake. "You just spoke to her, huh? Like dialin' 0800 SATOMI?"

Casey giggled, but Taylor wasn't amused. "Look, Blake, just trust me. I know it's weird, but we're a bunch of cyborgs inside an ancient alien space ship. Weird is our life now. So just go with it, okay?"

Blake didn't answer, and instead looked at Casey for support, but she was too busy spinning around in her chair to notice.

"Casey, start to approach the station, nice and easy, and let's see what happens," said Taylor, using Blake's silence as an opportunity to move things forward.

"Aye aye, Captain Taylor Ray," answered Casey, stopping her chair and then easing the Contingency One towards the Nexus.

"I don't believe this," moaned Blake, "the giant alien space fortress is expectin' us..." Then he turned back to face his console, muttering to himself, "But sure, why not... Let's just fly at a space station that could level a city in less time than it'd take me to neck a shot of bourbon, 'cause the voices in your head toldya to..."

Casey and Taylor both heard him clearly, thanks to their simulant hearing, and they glanced at each other, smiling. But then the mission ops console bleeped, wiping the smiles off both of their faces. Taylor rushed over to check it.

"That'd better be good news, Cap," Blake called over.

"Well, there's good news and there's bad news," said Taylor, checking the console, which had actually registered two separate alerts.

"Bad news first..." Blake called out.

This made Taylor smile again. *Always glass half-empty. At least he's consistent...* "The bad news is that another ship has just jumped in. Destroyer class. From the markings and drive signature, it's possibly even the same ship that appeared at the cave mouth of the Contingency base, before the larger Hedalt fleet arrived."

"That has to be more than just coincidence," said Casey. "Could it be Provost Adra? Maybe she tracked us somehow?"

Taylor rubbed his chin again, mulling the possibility over in his mind, but if it was Adra, why had she switched from a War Frigate to a vessel that was barely a match for their Corvette? "I don't know... maybe," said Taylor, "but I haven't entered the Fabric since the last time it nearly wiped me out, so I don't see how she could have tracked us here. And even if she had somehow managed that, why come here in a ship barely any more powerful than our own?"

"You know, those're great questions, Cap," said

Blake, "but how 'bout we don't hang around to find out?"

"You said there was good news?" Casey cut in, while also shooting Blake a reproving look.

"The good news is that the Nexus has sent us a message," said Taylor, "and you're not going to believe what it says."

"Try me..." said Blake.

"It says, 'Welcome home, Hunter AA-01. Proceed to Docking Section Alpha.' And it's even sent the co-ordinates," said Taylor, transferring the information to Casey's console.

"Got it, Cap, making my approach now," said Casey, throwing a thumbs up out to the side.

"I'm not sure whether that giant weapon talkin' to us makes me feel safer or just more weirded-out," said Blake, as the ship ascended towards a docking section near the center of the giant mass. Then Blake's console sounded an alert, and he read it anxiously, "The Destroyer is chargin' weapons and gainin' on us."

"Casey, I'm probably going to regret this, but can you go any faster?" asked Taylor, "The more of a head-start we can get over whoever that is, the better our chances of taking this thing down. And finding Satomi."

Casey smiled, and glanced back at Taylor as he sank back into his increasingly dented and bent command chair, "Are you asking me to land this thing as fast as I can?"

Taylor winced, knowing he'd regret what he was about to say, "I guess I am."

Casey let out an excited little whoop, and then pulled the pilot's viewport closer, "Aye, aye, Captain Taylor Ray!" She pulsed the ion engines and suddenly the image of the Nexus on the viewport began to rapidly enlarge.

Blake gripped the arms of his chair, terrified silver eyes fixed on the viewport and mouth twisted into a grimace, "Well, at least I can't hurl in this body," he called out, his tone rising as they hurtled towards the space station at a reckless speed. "So I guess that's somethin'!"

EIGHTEEN

In Earth Fleet military lingo, Casey's landing would have been described as 'sporty', which was a polite way of saying that it was little more than a controlled crash. However, Casey was no ordinary pilot. Despite approaching the hangar bay of the Nexus at more than twice the maximum speed that any normal pilot would attempt, she had somehow managed to wrestle the ship to a full stop and then drop them onto the deck with the softness of a feather landing.

Once Blake had recovered from the trauma of the experience, he had rushed off the bridge to the weapons store to make sure they were equipped for a confrontation. Casey's maneuver had given them a good head start over the Destroyer, but no-one doubted they'd be able to leave again without first facing the occupants of their Hedalt stalker.

At Taylor's command, Casey had left the reactor hot, so that they would be able to blast off again at a moment's notice, and then both had joined Blake, who had already laid out three sets of body armor and three sidearms.

Casey pulled on the armored jacket and then picked up and swiftly loaded one of the weapons. It was only after she had slipped the sidearm into her holster that she noticed Taylor wasn't with them. She looked around the corridor with a puzzled expression, "Where's the Cap?"

"He said he had to get somethin'," Blake replied, tightening the straps of his own armor. "I didn't ask why, but it looked like he was headed towards Satomi's quarters."

"Maybe he's looking for a memento," suggested Casey, but Blake just frowned and finished donning his armor. Casey shook her head at him, "You know, a personal item; something that might help to wake her up. He thinks there might be a Satomi on this station."

"Nah, that's not why he's ransackin' her quarters," said Blake, though the twinkle in his eyes suggested he was inviting Casey to ask, 'why?'.

"Go on, I'll bite," smirked Casey, "Why?"

"Well, he always did wanna get inside her drawers," Blake continued, with a wicked grin.

Casey laughed, "Blakey, I'm impressed," she beamed, "that might actually be the first time one of your smutty innuendos actually made sense!"

Blake's grin broadened, "I just hope the reason he's taking so long ain't 'cause he decided to put them on..."

"Put what on?" said Taylor, appearing behind Blake, as if he was a genie that had just been summoned with a magic word.

Blake shot bolt upright, and even though his simulant brow couldn't sweat and his simulant skin couldn't turn any paler than it already was, Taylor knew a guilty look when he saw one.

"Oh, nothin', Cap," said Blake, with a 'hand caught in the cookie jar' sort of nonchalance. "I was just sayin' to Casey that..." then he hesitated, realizing he had talked himself into a corner. He turned to Casey with imploring eyes, hoping she would be able to rescue him.

"He was just saying he hoped you weren't trying on Satomi's underwear," said Casey, totally deadpan.

"Casey, what the hell!" Blake exclaimed, then he turned to Taylor, "Cap, I didn't... I mean I wasn't..."

"Relax, Blake," said Taylor smiling, "you were actually correct, I *was* going through her drawers." Blake frowned again and then Taylor tapped his simulant ears. "I left the door open, so I couldn't help but overhear."

Blake seemed relieved, but then also slightly perplexed. He looked down at Taylor's pants, contemplating asking whether or not he'd actually guessed right.

"I was actually looking for this," Taylor continued, holding up a short length of twisted fabric with metal hooks at either end.

"What is it, Cap?" asked Casey, taking a step closer so she could get take the item from Taylor to get a better look.

"It's a trouser twist," said Taylor, as if the answer should have been obvious.

"A what-now?" said Blake and Casey in unison.

Taylor shook his head, "Maybe the Hedalt forgot to program that part of basic training into your brains," he said, snootily. "They help to keep the bottoms of your pants looking neat. They used to be part of the standard uniform regulations, but were phased out when the later uniforms came in," Then he grinned at Casey, "Not that you'd know, since following uniform code was never your forte..."

Casey shrugged and smiled back, "Well, since we were never officially part of Earth Fleet, strictly speaking I never flouted uniform regulations."

"A technicality," said Taylor, playing it straight, "it wouldn't hold up at court-martial..."

"And that's Satomi's special personal item?"

asked Blake, as Casey and Taylor laughed. He was still too caught up on how a trouser-twist could hold sentimental value. "I mean, what's so damn special 'bout it?"

"Well, it's kind of embarrassing..." Taylor began.

Blake looked at him like he was mad, "More embarrassing than me thinking you'd just slipped on a pair of her panties?"

"Well, no," said Taylor, wondering if Blake actually realized that simulants didn't need panties or any form of underwear. "It's silly really, but I lent her this one time when her hair band snapped, and she liked it so much she carried on using it."

"Aww, that's sweet, Cap," said Casey, cocking her head, but then Blake laughed and Casey had to back-hand him across the chest to shut him up. "But didn't that mean you had one leg untucked?"

"I had a spare, Casey!" said Taylor, also now laughing.

An auxiliary console on the wall of the corridor sounded an alert, which snapped them back to the reality of their situation faster than a shard of plasma. Blake checked the alert and relayed the information to the others, "Casey increased our lead over that Destroyer, but it's finally linin' up to dock. So we better move fast."

Taylor shoved the trouser-twist into his pocket and grabbed the last weapon and set of body armor off the deck, "Okay, let's get this done," he said, pressing the docking hatch release, which opened onto a short walkway that had extended after they landed. Taylor loaded the weapon and then looked at Blake and Casey, steely-eyed and serious. "I have no idea what to expect in there," he began, "but, I doubt we'll make it back out again without a fight. So I need you in game mode. We won't get another chance."

"Aye aye, Captain Taylor Ray," Casey replied, but with matching seriousness, instead of her usual breezy verve.

"You can count on me, Cap," said Blake, with gruff determination and a game-face to match. "Let's get Satomi an' blow this thing to hell."

They all ran out onto the hangar deck and headed towards a door at the far end.

"Where are we goin'?" asked Blake, drawing his weapon.

"Just keep your silver eyes peeled, we'll know it when we see it," said Taylor, hoping that Satomi would be true to her word.

"Great, I love a solid plan," complained Blake, sarcastically as they reached the door. He turned around to face the pursuing Hedalt ship approaching the outer airlock, "And what we do 'bout that Destroyer?"

"One thing at a time," replied Taylor, trying to open the door, "Casey, can you see a release anywhere?" Then, before she could answer, a vivid white glow surrounded the frame and the lights in the hangar dimmed.

"What the?..." said Blake as the door opened, leading on to a long corridor, which was pitch black, save for a row a white lights at floor level, which were pulsing, as if directing them to follow. Taylor stepped through the illuminated door frame and into the corridor and the realization of where he was smacked him in the face like a sucker punch.

It's the deep space corridor!... he said to himself, hardly believing his eyes. *The Nexus is the gateway, and I just passed through the starlight door in to the deep space corridor.*

"You okay, Cap?" asked Blake, noticing that Taylor seemed momentarily distracted.

"Follow the lights, people," said Taylor. "This place is where it all began for me. This is where it all connects. And this is where it's going to end."

NINETEEN

They advanced through the maze of corridors inside the Nexus, Taylor in the lead and Blake covering their rear, following the blinking lights at floor level like an electronic trail of breadcrumbs. They raced through sector after sector, most of which looked abandoned, except for the warm glow of console screens, and through others that were occupied by zombie-like simulants. Blake had cautiously raised his weapon to cover the various automatons, but they had simply moved back and forth between stations, performing their programmed duties, while ignoring the presence of Taylor and his crew.

Eventually, the pulsing white lights stopped at a large double-door, which to led into a laboratory or workshop area. Taylor stepped up and pressed the security access pad next to the door, but it was coded to only allow authorized personnel. *Knock, knock, Satomi, please let us in...* There was an anxious wait where seconds seemed like hours, then the doors slid open.

"I'll cover the door," said Blake, keenly aware that the occupants of the Destroyer would be closing in behind, "Try not to take too long doing whatever it is that you're doing." Then he glanced back at Taylor and smiled. "And try not to blow this damn thing up with us still inside."

"I'll do my best," said Taylor, though in truth he hadn't the faintest idea where to start.

"Hold it! Don't move!" cried Casey, and Taylor and Blake both spun around to see Casey aiming her weapon at a Hedalt male, dressed in a plain navy uniform.

The Hedalt dropped to his knees and held up his hands, "Don't shoot!" it cried back, hands shaking, "I'm not armed, I'm just an engineer."

Blake raced over and proficiently checked the engineer for weapons, finding none. "He's clean, Cap," he said, returning to cover the door. "Also, he ain't wearin' the armored getup that the soldiers all seem to wear, so maybe he's tellin' the truth."

"I am!" cried the engineer, "I am not part of Warfare Command, they just assigned me here!"

Taylor glanced over at Casey, who had already lowered her weapon, and then stepped closer to the engineer, who shuffled back until he bumped into the wall and then cowered lower. Taylor bent down and extended a hand, "We're not here to hurt you," he said, "What's your name?"

"Rikov," said the engineer, tentatively reaching up to accept Taylor's hand, which then hoisted him upright. "My name is Rikov." Then he saw Taylor properly for the first time, peering into his silver simulant eyes, before scanning the others in turn. "But, you are simulants!" he exclaimed. His shaky voice was now colored with a shade of excitement. "You are the high-functioning units. Hunters, correct?" He didn't wait for Taylor to answer, before adding, "But why are you here? Are you malfunctioning?"

"Ya could say that..." answered Blake, casually.

"I had been curious as to why the military officer from Warfare Command had visited her laboratory again after so long," Rikov continued, now oddly relaxed. "I thought that the Hunter Simulant Program had ended, but here you three are. Odd that I wasn't informed and that you are still in active mode. Where is the Satomi Rose unit? I should run the diagnostics on you as a collective."

"What officer?" asked Taylor, suddenly alert again. Blake heard it too and he arched his neck to peer through the windows, but the corridor was still clear. "Do you mean Adra?"

"How can you know that name?" asked Rikov, "You should not know her name. And you should not be in active consciousness mode." He reached into a pocket and brought out a data pad, which he held up to Taylor. "Let me check what has gone wrong."

"Look, Rikov, we're not your usual simulants," said Taylor, allowing Rikov to perform whatever analysis he was doing, "It would take too long to explain, but you need to get off this station."

Rikov's frown deepened, "I do not understand, your program does not register, and your neural activity is off the chart. I have never seen a simulant that is so..." he hesitated, unable to put into words what he was seeing.

"Alive?" suggested Taylor, and Rikov lowered the data pad and looked back at Taylor, once again full of fear.

"You are the rogue simulants..." he said, wide-eyed, "I had heard rumors, but did not believe they could be true."

"They're true," said Taylor. "We're real, and like I said, we're not here to hurt you. But I have to shut down the Nexus. I'll blow this thing out of space if I have to."

"But, why?" asked Rikov.

Taylor was starting to get frustrated. "Look, I don't have time to explain. A Hedalt Destroyer was following us in, and whoever is on board is probably looking for us."

"Captain!" Blake shouted over. "We're gonna have company very soon."

Then Casey stepped in and held Rikov gently by the shoulder, looking kindly into his terrified eyes, "Look, I'll give you the short-short version," she began, and her sociable tone seemed to relax Rikov. "A group of humans survived the war. We're helping them to take back Earth – to take back their home. But the only way they can do that is if we turn off this Nexus and disable all the simulants in the galaxy."

"Casey, he's Hedalt; I doubt helping humans is top of his agenda," said Taylor. He may have been stuck for a way forward, but he was confident that a Hedalt Engineer would not be sympathetic to their cause.

Rikov seemed astonished. "Not all Hedalt are like those in Warfare Command."

"Well, all the ones we've met have been," Blake called back. He was still paying attention, despite monitoring the hallway.

"You ask me to believe that you are different to other simulants, yet cannot accept not all Hedalt are warmongers?" asked Rikov, pluckily.

"Prove us wrong," said Taylor, hoping to gain an ally. "Help us."

"But how can I help?" asked Rikov. "All of the human bases were destroyed."

"You know about that?" said Taylor, now taking a turn to be astonished.

"Yes, I doubt there is a Hedalt alive who has not heard," said Rikov, "and of the incident at the Way Station and the attack on the reclamation facility. News of these events was classified, but of course everything is available on the CoreNet, if you know where to look."

"Don't believe everything you read on the CoreNet," Casey chipped in, cheerfully. "The human fleet survived. But they won't survive for much longer, unless we can turn this giant spaceball off."

"I will help you," said Rikov, which achieved the extraordinarily rare effect of stunning Casey into silence. "There are a great many among us who want nothing more than to see the authority of Warfare Command crumble," Rikov continued, speaking with passion and verve. "They have controlled our lives through fear and brutality for centuries, just as they once controlled you."

"Two armored freaks incomin', Cap," Blake shouted back, "Can ya save this li'l chit-chat for another time?"

"Casey, go help Blake," Taylor said, "keep them out of this room for as long as you can." He handed Casey his weapon and ammo clips, but in the process the trouser twist that he'd taken from Satomi's quarters fell from his pocket. None of them saw it land on the deck and fall through the thin metal grates.

"Aye aye, Captain Taylor Ray," said Casey, taking the weapon and holstering it so that she could slide the extra clips into the pouches on her body armor. "Don't take too long!" she added, before sprinting over to join Blake.

Rikov grabbed Taylor by the cuff of his jacket and ushered him over to one of the workstations. "I can trigger the laboratory to go into emergency containment mode. Even the Provost will not be able to override it. It will give you some time!" He began working the console as shots rang out behind them; Blake and Casey had smashed the glass in the doorway and were firing along the corridor to suppress the advancing Hedalt soldiers. Taylor hadn't seen their faces, but he knew Adra must have been one of them. "There, done!" cried Rikov, then shutters slammed down over the exits, including the door that Blake and Casey were defending. "We will be safe in here for now."

"Can you also shut down this station?" asked Taylor, grateful for his new friend's intervention. "We need to disable all the simulants if Earth Fleet is to have any chance against Warfare Command's armada."

Rikov shook his head, "No, I do not have that kind of access. I doubt even the High Provost would be able to trigger such an event – disabling the Nexus would cripple the empire."

"Then how do we shut it down?" wondered Taylor, asking the question more to himself than to Rikov. *Come on, Satomi, help me out! What's the next step?*

"There is no way to shut down the Nexus," Rikov answered, becoming flustered again, "The Nexus has existed for countless millennia. It was built by the Masters, long before the Hedaltus were brought to the world below."

"The Masters?"

"The beings that brought us here from our original home planet," said Rikov, surprised that Taylor was ignorant of this fact. "The beings that created the frame you now inhabit, and which created the CoreNet and Fabric itself."

"I guess there's a lot I still don't know," Taylor admitted, "but right now, all I need to know is how to shut this thing down."

"Besides an assault from a thousand warships, disabling its power source is the only way," Rikov offered. "The Nexus pulls energy from the Fabric itself, drawing it through like a black hole sucks in light itself."

"Great, so how do we turn it off, or destroy it?"

"You cannot," said Rikov without hesitation, "It is impossible. No living creature can get near the core, not even you."

Damn it, Taylor, think! There has to be a way!
Then he remembered how he had been able to
influence and direct energy while connected to the
Fabric. He'd done it several times before, on the
Way Station and at the reclamation facility. "Is
there a way for me to hook into the CoreNet from
here?" Taylor asked, feeling a tingle of excitement
inside his simulant skull. "If I can connect to the
CoreNet, I might be able to overload the core."

"How?..." Rikov began, but Taylor held up his
hand.

"There's no time to explain," he said, though he
also couldn't explain even if he wanted to. "Is there
a way?"

"Yes, I believe so," Rikov answered. "The
original simulant stasis pods all have direct neural
interfaces." Then he pointed towards a large open
space at the far side of the laboratory. "The original
prototypes are still inside too. This is where the
military officer first created them."

"The original prototypes of what?" said Taylor,
scrunching up his simulant brow.

"Of you, of course," said Rikov, again speaking
as if Taylor should have known this. "Casey Valera,
Blake Meade, Taylor Ray and..."

"Satomi Rose..." said Taylor out loud. Suddenly,
everything was becoming clear; how he had been
able to see Satomi and she him, and how they had
communicated all this time. He looked towards

the large open chamber and suddenly recognized it. It was the same space he had seen during the extraordinary long jump to the Nexus.

"Come on!" he called to Rikov, and then his simulant legs propelled him towards the stasis pods at the far end of the chamber at a speed that made an Olympic 100m sprinter look slow. Hurriedly, he checked the names on the console screen and then peered inside each pod. *Casey Valera... non-viable, Blake Meade... non-viable, Taylor Ray... non-viable. Just like I saw during the jump!* He thought. And then he saw her. Satomi Rose. He double-checked the status... *Unit viable.* She was still alive! Alive, but in stasis.

Taylor accessed the console and rapidly worked through the settings, until he finally managed to unlock the pod and deactivate the stasis field. Tearing the door off the chamber, he tossed it aside, as if it were nothing more substantial than balsa wood, and then waited as the figure inside began to rouse and then unsteadily stumble towards him. Taylor caught Satomi and hoisted her back to her feet as her silver simulant eyes opened and registered him for the first time.

"Satomi!" Taylor cried, "Satomi, can you hear me? Do you know who I am?"

Satomi looked at him, studying his smooth simulant face, "What's happening?" she said, her words coming out as an electronically-processed slur. "You look strange..." Then Satomi looked around the large open chamber, "Where am I? I can't feel myself breathing. Taylor, what's going on?"

"It's okay, Satomi," said Taylor, trying to comfort her as best he could, but there was no DMZ to fall back on here. Satomi was waking up to a new reality and seeing it raw and unfiltered, just as Taylor had done on the Contingency Base.

Then he remembered the trouser twist, "Wait, I have something that will help!" he cried, and reached into his jacket pocket, but he felt nothing but the fabric lining. He fumbled around for several seconds looking for the twist, but then to his horror he realized it was no longer there.

TWENTY

Taylor panicked. The trouser twist may not have seemed like much, but it was a vital link between the fictional reality the Hedalt had programmed into Satomi's brain through the advanced neural circuitry and the real world. That the object had existed in both the programmed reality and the real world somehow connected these two existences like a bridge. It allowed the mind to step through the looking glass and not only escape the fictional reality, but more rapidly come to terms with the truth. Without it, Taylor had no way to help Satomi adjust, and he still desperately needed her help. But time was running out.

"Taylor what's wrong with my hands?!" Satomi cried, "And what happened to your face! You don't look..." she couldn't finish the sentence and forced her eyes shut.

"I'm not human, Satomi," said Taylor, guessing what she was about to say. "But I *am* real. Try to remember. You came to me, and told me to come here, to the Nexus. Don't you remember?"

"I... I can't remember..." said Satomi, and then her voice broke down into a garble of electronic sound, like an old fashioned cassette tape being played on rewind. "I... what's happening... to me... Taylor... please..."

"Satomi look at me!" cried Taylor. He was having to physically hold her upright; if he let go, she would have collapsed to the deck. "Look at me, please!"

Satomi's head jerked upright and Taylor slid his hand gently behind her head to support it. Slowly, she eased open her silver simulant eyes. "I'm real, Satomi. This frame is just a shell, but inside it's still Taylor. And you're still Satomi." Their eyes locked and then Satomi's body started to feel stronger. She traced the outline of his face with her eyes, scanning the line of his chin and the shape of his nose, then suddenly she reached up and placed a hand against his cheek. Taylor smiled, realizing what had just happened. He was the object that Satomi had a connection to; he was her touchstone of reality.

"Taylor?" she said, her voice now returning to

normal. Her balance was now steadier and she managed to stand, unaided. "You're here? When did you arrive?"

"Not long ago. Thanks for opening the door and leading the way here."

"It's like I'm waking from a dream, but the dream was real," said Satomi, rubbing her eyes. And then she realized that Taylor's hand was on the back of her head, with the other clasped around her waist. "Were we just... kissing?"

Taylor couldn't help it; he laughed out loud, almost maniacally, and then released Satomi and took a pace back, "No, but in all honestly, Satomi, I *could* kiss you right now."

Satomi rubbed the back of her neck and looked away, "Yes, well, I think we have other matters to resolve first."

"My thoughts exactly," replied Taylor, still grinning like a loon. Satomi's transition had been quicker even than Blake's, but in truth Satomi had been adjusting to what she was from the first moment they had talked inside the Fabric, what seemed like a lifetime ago. "But we're running out of time. Casey and Blake are over by the door. One of the engineers helped to seal us inside, but there are two Hedalt military officers outside, and I don't know how long we can keep them out for."

"Vice Provost Adra and Adjutant Vika," said Satomi, nodding.

"Vice Provost?" said Taylor, picking up on the change of title. "The last time we saw her, she was a Provost and her adjutant was someone called Lux."

"Let's just say her fortunes have dwindled since then," replied Satomi, "but that only makes her more desperate. And dangerous."

Taylor saw that Blake and Casey appeared to have noticed Satomi, and were running in their direction. He turned back to Satomi with a million questions on his mind, but he spoke the only one that mattered. "Do you know how to disable the Nexus?" he asked, "I thought perhaps I could overload the power core, using one of these stasis chambers."

"Great minds think alike," said Satomi, smiling, "but, you can't do it alone, Taylor. The effort would kill you."

"Then how? I assume you know a way?"

"I do," said Satomi as Blake and Casey arrived, giddy expressions on their faces. Casey wasted no time and threw herself onto Satomi, embracing her like a long-lost sister, while Blake stood alongside Taylor, awkwardly trying to hide his obvious joy at seeing their Technical Specialist again.

"How do you feel?" asked Casey, eventually pulling back and beaming at her, "I can't believe you're here!"

"I'll tell you everything later, Casey," said

Satomi, "but first, I need your help." Then she looked at Taylor and Blake too. "I need all of you. Or, more precisely, Taylor does."

"What d'ya need, Satomi?" asked Blake. "Just name it."

"It's going to sound a little crazy, but I need you all to get inside these stasis pods," Satomi said, gesturing to the four tubes behind her. "From here, Taylor and I can hook into the CoreNet and overload the power core."

"You gottit," said Blake, "but Casey and I can't dial-in like Taylor can. What're we s'posed to do in there?"

"You can't connect to the CoreNet, but we can connect to each other," said Satomi. "Disabling the CoreNet will take all four of us. We'll need to draw from your strength."

Rikov also now came running over and for a moment he didn't realize that there was a new addition to the simulant troupe. "The Vice Provost, I believe she is planting charges around the door!" Rikov blurted out. And then he saw Satomi, and the empty chamber behind her. "But that is simply not possible!" he began, rushing to her and inspecting her like a technician inspecting a priceless piece of machinery. Then he changed his mind, "No, this is more than impossible – it's incredible! You are the AA0 model, but you have been non-viable for centuries. How are you..."

"Alive?" finished Satomi, smiling at him. Then she looked at Taylor and gave a little shrug, "I guess not everything can be explained with science or logic. Some things I suppose just... are."

Blake snorted, "Okay, tell us what you have done with the real Satomi?"

They all laughed, but then a series of low vibrations originating from the direction of the sealed doorway brought them sharply back to reality.

"Empty the other chambers, quickly," said Satomi, "If Adra gets inside this laboratory, we lose our chance."

"I'm more concerned about her killing us first," Taylor chipped in, but then he joined Blake and Casey as they each opened one of the remaining stasis chambers. Respectfully, they removed their non-viable doppelgangers and delicately rested their bodies on the deck to the side. Taylor had gotten used to seeing his simulant reflection, but handling what was essentially a dead version of himself was high amongst the more bizarre and chilling events he'd experienced.

Casey had been more concerned at the lack of color or creativity in her double's clothing, while Blake had pulled a face like was chewing a wasp the whole time he was wrestling non-viable Blake to the deck.

"Rikov, if this works then you'll need to get off

this station, fast," said Taylor, stepping inside his chamber. "Do you have any way to escape?"

Rikov nodded, "There are planetary shuttles that can take the crews back down to the surface of the home world," he answered, "enough to get everyone away. Once you destabilize the power core, the emergency evacuation protocols will kick in automatically. I will be fine, but until then, I shall do my best to keep the soldiers out."

Rikov turned to head back into the main laboratory, but Taylor called out to stop him. In all the time he'd been awake, he'd never considered that there could be more to the Hedalt race than the cruel and belligerent warriors of Warfare Command, or the equally menacing racketeers. But Rikov had opened his eyes to another reality that was just as startling as his own. As he had once been under the control of Warfare Command, so too it appeared were the majority of Hedalt society, forced to live under the strict rule of the empire. Perhaps destroying the Nexus and crippling simulants throughout the galaxy would not only deliver justice for the crimes committed against humanity, but it would liberate the Hedalt people too. Rikov frowned as he waited for Taylor to eventually speak, but there was too much to say and so he kept it brief.

"Thank you."

Rikov seemed to understand the layers of

meaning hidden inside those two simple words. He bowed slightly, maintaining eye contact with Taylor, before hurrying away. Taylor realized that there were times when simply saying 'thank you', and meaning it with a deep sincerity, could be more powerful than a thousand words.

"Is everyone ready?" Satomi called out.

"Ready when you are..." Taylor answered.

"Aye aye, Technical Specialist Satomi Rose!" said Casey with her usual gusto.

"Hell no..." said Blake.

Then the chamber collapsed in around them and they all fell through normal space and into a state of nothingness, into a void similar to what they experienced during a jump. For a few seconds there was nothing and then they each emerged again inside an opaque corridor, surrounded by stars. But this space was different to the one that Taylor knew. Instead of a single corridor, there were four, intersecting in the center to form a cross. Each corridor had a doorway, and unlike the closed door of the DMZ, all four were open. But where the door frames in front of Casey and Blake were dull and absent of light and color, the ones in front of Taylor and Satomi were bathed in an iridescent glow. These were starlight doors, Taylor understood. The gateways into the Fabric.

Taylor was the first to run through, followed quickly by Satomi, but instead of being surrounded by an endless system of wire-framed cubes that seemed to extend into infinity around him, Taylor was surrounded by what seemed to be millions of pinpricks of light, with himself and Satomi at the very center.

"This is the Nexus, Taylor," said Satomi. "This is where the Fabric begins, and this is where it ends. Every thread connects to this one point. Every command, message and response that Warfare Command has ever issued and will ever issue originates and ends here. It's what brought us together."

Taylor was awestruck by the immense beauty of what he was seeing, but then something about what Satomi had said gave him chills. He'd forgotten that inside the Fabric, he was capable of physical emotion again. "If we destroy the Nexus, what happens to us?" he asked, "I know we've broken free of the Hedalt programming, but we're still simulants. If the Nexus is destroyed, are we destroyed with it?"

Satomi took Taylor's hands, and the warmth of her touch took him completely by surprise. His simulant hands could detect temperature and pressure, but the touch of a human hand was something uniquely special. "I don't have all the answers Taylor," Satomi admitted, "but I do know that if we don't destroy the Nexus, we'll never truly be free. Don't ask me how I know that; I just know."

Taylor smiled and squeezed her hands gently, "I'm going to have to get used to this new, open-minded Satomi Rose. I thought you were guided by tech manuals and formulae."

Satomi smiled back, "Maybe the original Satomi Rose was," she said, "but I'm someone different. And so are you."

"I'd like to figure out who these two new people are," said Taylor, and then he forced himself to lock his gaze onto hers, even though all he wanted was to look away, "and it would be great if we could figure it out together."

Satomi laughed, which was not the reaction Taylor had expected, or, if he was honest, had hoped for. But then she touched her hand to the side of his face, as she had done only minutes earlier, except this time the feeling was electric. "Here we are, about to bring our whole universe crashing down around us, and you choose this moment to hit on me?"

Taylor laughed and then shrugged, "Sorry, I guess I never really knew what to say, or when."

"I wouldn't be so sure," said Satomi, and then she kissed him softly on the lips. It perhaps only lasted for a second or two, but to Taylor it felt like an eternity. "Are you ready?"

"I'm ready."

They closed their eyes, still holding each other's

hands tightly, and focused on the Nexus, concentrating on the source of its power; the rift between normal space and the Fabric that had been torn open by the Masters eons ago. They both felt it instantly and were drawn to it. Together, they began to fly through the Fabric, deep into the belly of the Nexus, into its heart. The corridors remained connected, pulling Casey and Blake with them. And just as they could sense their presence in the void of a super-luminal jump, Taylor and Satomi could feel them now. Casey and Blake were linked to them, through their consciousness and energy. It was a connection stronger than any metal, a bond stronger than friendship, stronger even than blood. In that moment, they were all one.

Taylor opened his eyes and was almost blinded by the intensity of the light that penetrated the space around them, like the light from a star focused through a diamond. "I can see it!" cried Taylor, "What do we do?"

"You know what to do, Taylor," said Satomi "You've done it before. Just concentrate. I'm with you!"

Taylor took a deep breath and squeezed Satomi's hands even more tightly, so tightly he was worried he might hurt her, but Satomi just squeezed back. Knowing she was there with him this time filled him with the confidence he needed.

He closed his eyes again and pictured the Nexus' power core in his mind. *Overload...*

As soon as he thought the word, he heard it echo back to him, and then he heard Satomi repeat it too, their thoughts blending together as one. Pain reached out and crippled his body, ten times more intense than any pain he'd felt before; even more intense than Provost Adra's purge that had almost destroyed him. He felt his grip weaken, and despite Satomi's hold on him, the pain was too intense and he could feel himself slipping away. Then two more pairs of hands clasped around him, simultaneously pulling him back up and also keeping him rooted. He opened his eyes and saw Blake and Casey, but it was like looking at a reflection of them in a window, as if there weren't really there.

"Keep trying!" cried Satomi, her voice distorted and muddled. "We've got you!"

He could barely make her out through the blinding light that filled the void between them. But he was no longer afraid, or unsure of their success. He knew that together – as a crew, as a family – they could succeed. He shut his eyes again. *Overload...*

Suddenly, the light faded and fractured, as if the diamond lens had cracked. He opened his eyes and saw Satomi clearly, still holding his hands.

"We've done it!" cried Satomi, "The power core

is destabilizing, The Nexus will be destroyed. We have to leave!"

Together they were flying again, back through the guts of the Nexus and into deep space, still as a connected quartet of corridors, until they were back to where they had begun.

Satomi released Taylor's hands and slapped him on the chest, "Go! Run back through the door!"

Then without another word she was running away from him, towards her own starlight door. Taylor turned and ran too and together they passed through the threshold and out into the void of nothingness, where all that existed was their consciousness, and then finally back into the real world inside the Nexus.

Taylor stepped out of the stasis chamber and onto the deck plating, which was shuddering with seismic-like tremors. Alarms were ringing out all around and the lights were flickering chaotically. He looked along the broad, open hall and saw a figure lying on the deck. He ran towards it with the others close behind and quickly realized that the body was that of the Hedalt engineer, Rikov. His torso was twisted and contorted and his head had been wrenched almost one hundred and eighty degrees around. Taylor looked up and saw a blackened and jagged opening where the laboratory door had once been, and then from the flickering shadows to his side he saw two figures move. One was a Hedalt officer he had never seen before, but the other face he could never forget. It was Adra.

"Avoid this purge, simulant..." Adra snarled. Then she raised her plasma pistol and shot Taylor in the chest.

TWENTY-ONE

Taylor looked down at the smoldering hole in his chest. He could taste the acrid fumes of burning polymers and scorched circuity, but the lack of pain was confusing and surreal, as if the wound was an illusion.

He staggered backwards, suddenly losing control of his legs, but strong arms caught him and prevented his fall. He managed to tilt his head back to see Satomi supporting him, looking more scared than he'd ever seen her before. Her mouth was moving, like she was yelling or even screaming, but he couldn't hear her. Only the sound of the plasma pistol discharging resonated in his ears, blocking everything else out.

Blake turned to make a run for his weapon, which was lying on the floor, beside his non-functional simulant counterpart, but the ripple of plasma filled the air again and the shard struck the deck beside him. Blake froze and glowered back at Vice Provost Adra, smoking pistol in hand, face twisted with a mixture of disgust and satisfaction.

"Try that again, and the next shot will be to your head, simulant," Adra challenged, snarling the word 'simulant'. "I intend for you all to die in due course, but not until you have watched your precious Captain expire first."

"You're too late!" Blake growled back at her, "This place is gonna blow an' take us all with it!"

Adra's right eye twitched and then she shot a glance back to Vika, who understood the subtle message and removed a data pad from her coat pocket. Several seconds passed with only the piercing shriek of the evacuation alarms breaking the silence, until Vika lowered the data pad to her side and slowly stepped beside Adra.

"The simulant is correct," said Vika. She moderated the volume of her voice with the intention that the simulants couldn't hear, but she hadn't accounted for their heightened senses. "The power core is destabilizing."

"Impossible," growled Adra, snatching the pad from her grasp with her spare hand. She read the information, digging deeper into the systems menu, but all she discovered was that Vika was correct. The power core was destabilizing and there was nothing she could do about it. Even as a full provost, she would require a quorum of Warfare Council members even to access such a critical system. As a vice provost she was powerless to intervene.

"Leave!" Satomi called out. She had sunk to her knees, still cradling Taylor's body in her arms with his silver eyes staring up at her, growing duller with each passing second. "It doesn't matter what you do to us anymore. Your fleet will be crippled and Earth will fall to the humans. You have lost!"

"We will crush your pitiful fleet, even without simulants!" Adra growled, while thrusting the data pad back towards Vika, without even bothering to look at her. Had she done so, Adra would have seen the burning hostility in the adjutant's eyes; hostility that had not gone unnoticed by Satomi or the others. "Return to the ship and compute a course to Earth," Adra barked, still waiting for Vika to take the data pad from her. "I will join you once I have destroyed these abominations!"

Vika took the data pad and tossed it to the deck behind her, like a piece of trash. The sound of the device clattering and scraping across the metal caused Adra to jerk around, in case there was another simulant she'd missed. When she saw the pad on the deck, she raised her eyes to meet Vika's.

"I am no longer yours to command," Vika said, the words seeping out of her mouth like venom,

"The simulant is correct – you have failed. Earth is lost. And your life is now mine to take!"

Satomi, Blake and Casey watched in stunned silence as the two Hedalt soldiers squared off and began to slowly circle one another, eyes locked. Both were coiled and ready to strike. If they'd had lungs, each of the simulants would have been holding their breath.

Adra struck first, raising her plasma pistol to shoot Vika at point-blank range, but Vika was ready. Stepping in, she stripped the pistol from Adra's grasp, before throwing a fast jab that the Vice Provost blocked with equally astonishing speed. Vika pressed her advantage, pushing Adra back with an unrelenting succession of powerful strikes that even Adra was unable to defend against. Taking hits to the face and body, Adra staggered back, feeling the pain register, despite the protection of her armor. But Vika was overconfident and overstretched, allowing Adra to deflect her next assault and open up a space between them; enough for her to recover her footing.

"I love a good fight," said Blake as the melee continued, with Adra and Vika trading blow for blow, neither gaining a clear upper hand over the other, "but how 'bout we get the hell outta here while they're tryin' to kill each other?"

"What about Taylor?" cried Satomi. "We can't

leave him!"

"We ain't leavin' no-one," boomed Blake, "Sonner'll fix him, but we have to get outta here first. Now c'mon, while we still can!"

Casey helped Satomi hoist Taylor over her shoulder in a fireman's lift and then they all began to edge along the side of the chamber as discreetly as possible.

But then Casey suddenly stopped. "Wait, I have an idea!"

"Casey, what the hell?!" Blake called back, as Casey ran in the opposite direction towards the four empty stasis pods. He cursed and then turned to Satomi, "Get the ship fired up. I'll catch ya up, once our damn pilot comes back!"

"Hurry!" Satomi called back, "this station will tear itself apart in minutes!"

Blake nodded, and then watched to make sure that Satomi made it past the warring Hedalt duo, who were still locked in a furious hand-to-hand engagement. Blood was smeared across both of their faces and each was showing signs of fatigue. But Blake knew that a wounded animal could be even more dangerous, and did not want to be around to confront whoever emerged the victor.

Keeping half an eye on the fight, Blake looked back to see Casey now running back towards him, carrying a body over her shoulder. When she got closer, he could see that it was the prototype simulant frame of Taylor Ray.

"What the hell are ya doin' with that?" asked Blake, looking at her as if she were crazy.

"Spare parts, knucklehead," replied Casey, "The Cap needs a new body, right?"

"Oh, hey, you're smarter than ya look!" said Blake, and Casey kicked him in the shins, "Ow!" he yelped, even though he felt no pain, "Now run, will ya? I got your back!"

Casey set off, but had to slam on the brakes as Adra and Vika tore in front of her and hammered into the wall. Their hands were at each other's throats, and both were still too consumed with trying to kill one other to notice Casey or Blake.

"Go round!" called out Blake, shielding her as she carried the limp simulant body into the middle of the chamber.

Adra and Vika remained locked together, neither giving an inch to the other. The fight had descended from a contest of combat skill into a brutal brawl for survival. It had come down to who had the greater will to survive. Vika's thirst for revenge versus Adra's refusal to let the humans win, at any cost.

"I lied to you..." spluttered Adra, fighting for breath as Vika's nails dug into her skin. "In the end... Lux had... my respect... You will die... with nothing..."

Vika's bloodied eyes quivered and her pupils

constricted, "You did not... deserve... his loyalty!" she gasped back at her, showering Adra's face with speckles of bright-red blood.

Vika's emotional outburst was all that Adra needed, because in that split-second her grip had weakened. It was only by a fraction, but a fraction was all that separated them. Breaking Vika's hold, Adra then smashed a forearm into her throat, causing the Adjutant to crumble to her knees, hands clasped to her neck, unable to breathe.

Adra took a step back and stared down at her, before drawing the black blade from inside her coat. "You know nothing of loyalty," she hissed, before spitting blood at Vika's feet. Vika looked up, eyes still full of hatred, and Adra launched a kick to her head, sending it bouncing off the metal wall like a football, before her body fell to the deck. A slowly expanding pool of blood started to grow around Vika's fractured skull.

Adra knelt by her side with the grace of someone who was about to pray, and held Vika's jaw, forcing the Adjutant to look into her eyes. "You had the chance to be great," said Adra, with contempt, "the chance to be something special. But look at you now." She shook her head in disgust and then plunged the blade into Vika's throat, angling it up towards the back of her skull. She watched the life leak out of Vika's body, as the Adjutant reached up and grabbed Adra's arm in a pitiful and futile attempt to push her away. "I will claim what is rightfully mine," Adra continued, "no-one will stand in my way." Then she pulled the knife out of Vika's flesh and rose imperiously back to her full height. It was then that she saw Casey Valera, a simulant body draped over her shoulder. She recognized it instantly as the body of the one being she detested more than any other in the galaxy, even more than any human. The body of Captain Taylor Ray.

"Oh no," snarled Adra, angling the blood-soaked blade towards Casey, "You do not get to leave!"

Suddenly Adra was hit from the side by a full speed tackle from Blake, which knocked her to the deck and sent them both spiraling out of control.

"Blake!" Casey cried out, as he tumbled across the floor with Adra close beside him. "Blake!"

"Just go, Casey!" Blake called back, climbing to his knees as Adra rose alongside him, face blooded and bruised and twisted with rage. "I'll catch you up!"

"I'm going to enjoy breaking you, simulant!" snarled Adra, who had managed to hold on to her blade, despite the fall. "I will slice you apart piece by piece while you watch. And then... then I will start on your friend." Adra flicked the tip of the blade towards Casey, who was still frozen like a statue with Taylor over her shoulder, face drawn and eyes wide.

"Give it ya best shot, steel skin!" Blake snapped back, inviting Adra on with a cocky wave of his hand. But whereas Vika or a human would have been susceptible to Adra's taunts, Blake's fury was contained in his mind. A fully-human Blake Meade would have succumbed to her threats and launched a frenzied charge at Adra, letting the anger flow uncontrollably through his fists and elbows and feet. A fully-human Blake Meade would have succumbed to blind rage, as Vika had done. And, as a consequence, a fully-human Blake Meade would have been dead in seconds. But this Blake Meade was not fully human. He was unique. And he wasn't about to fall into Adra's trap.

Blake advanced and feigned an attack, drawing Adra forward, blade pressed towards where his human heart would have been. But his deception had caused Adra to commit and overextend, and as he caught her by the wrist and twisted it into a lock, he saw fear flash into her severe green eyes for the first time.

"See, you ain't all that..." said Blake, coolly, before slamming the palm of his hand into her chest, catapulting her across the room and into the wall as if she'd been hit by a cannon blast. Adra fell, face pressed against the deck, next to the lifeless body of Adjutant Vika.

The entire laboratory then shook with the force

of an earthquake. Consoles exploded all around him and fissures began to open up in the walls and deck plating. Blake saw Casey, still waiting for him by the doorway, waving him on, though her voice was lost in the maelstrom of explosions that were erupting around him. He took one last look at Vice Provost Adra, lying motionless on the deck, and then ran for his life, back towards Casey.

TWENTY-TWO

Casey blasted out of the docking section with a controlled burst from the main ion engines, sending them rocketing into space like a torpedo. Switching to a reverse angle on the viewport, the Nexus shrank rapidly into the distance, set against the backdrop of a steel-gray planet. Electrical arcs and fiery explosions large enough to engulf entire starships were erupting all over the surface.

As Casey watched, she was able to make out dozens of interplanetary shuttles soaring out, like bees leaving a hive, carrying the Hedalt engineers to the home world below. She thought of Rikov and how without his sacrifice they would not have had time to execute the core overload. It seemed so cruelly unfair that he would perish, while the others, oblivious to his heroism, would survive to see their military overlords stripped of their key weapon of control. Without simulants, perhaps there would be an uprising. She hoped so, but thoughts of the future would have to wait. There was still the battle for Earth to fight, and they couldn't do that without their captain.

A blinding flash of light saturated the viewport, causing it to polarize to reduce the intensity, and then the Nexus was gone. Casey had never seen a star go supernova, but she imaged that it might have looked similar. But instead of a black hole forming where the Nexus once was, there remained only dust and fiery debris. The tear between normal space and the Fabric was gone.

Casey set the Contingency One to autopilot, sprang out of her chair and ran down the corridor to the workshop, where they'd unceremoniously dumped the wounded body of Taylor Ray and the prototype frame, before blasting off. She burst through the door to find Satomi, datapad in hand, rapidly assessing Taylor's injured body, and Blake to the side, arms folded, brow wrinkled with concerned lines.

"How is he?" asked Casey, running to the side of the workbench.

"His core power systems are shutting down," said Satomi, placing the datapad down, "His brain will die if we don't replace his body within the next few minutes."

"What if we shoved his head back into the cubby hole in his quarters?" suggested Blake. "You know, the place they kept our heads, before we woke up?"

"Good idea, but in order to detach the cranial unit, the neural interfaces first need to switch to a subconscious mode," said Satomi. "Sort of like putting a computer into sleep mode, where it's turned off, but still active at a low level."

"He looks kinda asleep to me?" said Blake, looking at the unconscious form of his captain.

"He's disabled, not asleep," said Satomi, while working to release the fastenings that held Taylor's cranial unit in place. "We need to quickly switch his head with the prototype frame that Casey brought back, and hope that he stabilizes."

"Hope ain't a good strategy, Satomi," grumbled Blake, "that body was holed up doin' nothin' for centuries; we don't even know if it still works."

"The frame is fully-functional," said Satomi, confidently, finishing the adjustments to Taylor's body so that his head was ready to detach. "I know, because my body is functional. The stasis fields built into the chambers are able to maintain the core circuitry and power systems of a simulant almost indefinitely. Organic components fare less well."

"Okay, so we stick his head on this body, and he'll be fine, right?" said Blake. "So, let's just get on with it already."

Satomi knew that Blake's brusque manner was simply due to worry and anxiety; she was worried too. "Blake, the short and honest answer is, I don't know what will happen, okay?" Externally, Satomi was calm thanks to her simulant frame, but her mind was racing in a hundred different directions. "So if you want to help, stop asking questions and put the prototype frame on the workbench next to Taylor."

Relived to finally have something to do, Blake snapped into action, grabbing the prototype Taylor Ray and sliding it alongside the Captain. Satomi sprang around to the opposite side of the workbench and rapidly repeated the procedure she'd just performed on their Taylor to detach the cranial unit on the prototype.

"Okay, this is going to take all three of us," said Satomi as she finished the adjustments to the prototype. "Casey, stand in front of Taylor and place your hands on the sides of his head. Blake, do the same for this one." They both raced into position, practically colliding with each other in their haste to take up their positions. "Then on the count of three, I need you both to remove the cranial units at the same time." She then locked eyes with Casey, "Casey, it's then your job to attach Taylor's head to the prototype as rapidly as you can. Once it's inserted, I'll try to power up the frame." Casey nodded frantically, clearly terrified by the vital importance of her role, but equally as determined to do her job.

"What about me?" said Blake.

"One you have the prototype head, just get the hell out of Casey's way, okay?" replied Satomi.

"Roger that," said Blake, relieved that his role was a lot simpler than Casey's. But, in truth, he trusted no-one more than Casey to complete the task. Her unique pilot's instincts and surgically-precise hands made her perfect for the job. But then he had a thought, "Why not just yank the head off this prototype first, so it's all ready to go?"

"Because I want the switch to be near instantaneous;" explained Satomi, "I want the prototype body to think the swap was just a glitch. Hopefully, it will then accept the new head and simply adjust for the glitch, without even realizing." Then she threw her arms out to the side, "Hell, guys, I'm just making this up as I go along. This isn't science, it's more like..."

"Going out on a wing and a prayer?" suggested Casey.

"Exactly."

"Don't worry, Satomi," continued Casey, smiling weakly, "We're used to winging it by now. And so is the Cap. He'll be fine."

Satomi smiled and nodded, "Okay then, is everyone ready?" Casey and Blake grasped the two heads and waited.

"Go in five...

...Four

...Three

...Two

...One!

Blake yanked the head off the prototype unit and practically leaped backwards, colliding with the workshop wall and leaving a shoulder-shaped dent in it, but before his feet had even touched the deck again, Casey had already placed Taylor's head onto the prototype body. It was a literal 'blink and you'd miss it' switch.

Satomi had pushed power into the prototype frame at the exact moment Casey had inserted the head, zapping it with electricity like a defibrillator. She then grabbed the data pad, ready to analyze the newly joined combination, but before she even touched the screen, Taylor sat bolt upright.

"I've been shot!" he yelled so loudly that everyone else in the room jumped in surprise. Then he looked down, pressing his hands to his chest and realizing that he hadn't in fact been shot and his panicked expression switched to one of deep confusion. "I haven't been shot..." he commented, "that's weird..." Then he looked at Satomi, and then at Casey and Blake, and then back at his own body. "What happened to Adra and the Nexus? Why are we all back on the ship? And why have you changed my clothes?"

"Taylor, relax," said Satomi, resting a reassuring hand on his shoulder, while also closing the fixings to ensure the Captain's head didn't literally fall off, "you're safe. But, to answer your questions, Adra and Vika fought, and Vika was killed. I carried you back here, while Blake took care of Adra." Taylor looked at Blake wide-eyed.

"What can I say, Cap, I'm just that good," he said with a broad grin.

"Casey then grabbed the prototype Taylor Ray and brought it to the ship, before blasting out of the Nexus using a burst from the ion engines," Satomi paused and looked over at the grinning pilot. "An incredibly risky maneuver that flies in the face of in-station piloting regulations..."

"What can I say, Cap, I'm just that good," said Casey, deliberately parroting Blake's cocky delivery.

"Then the Nexus exploded," Satomi continued, "and we brought you here, where we switched your head onto the body of the prototype Taylor Ray." Satomi paused again, trying to think if she'd missed anything, "I think that pretty much sums it up. Any questions?"

Taylor laughed, and then looked at his new body again, flexing his fingers and testing every joint and synthetic muscle, "I feel exactly the same," he commented after a few seconds. "You guys really are something else."

He jumped off the workbench, where Casey was waiting for him with a hug, and then he shook the hand of Blake, who looked deeply embarrassed at even this level of physical contact and show of emotion, before he moved around the workbench to Satomi. They stood opposite one other, awkwardly trying to work out what to do, before Blake chimed in, "Just hug or kiss or somethin'... The tension is killing us!"

Everyone laughed and then Satomi shrugged, "Let's just try a hug shall we?"

Taylor shrugged back, "I'm sure this is against Earth Fleet regulations too, but what the hell," then he moved forward and wrapped his arms around her. He couldn't feel the warmth of her comfort in the same way a human could, but there was still something pure about a simple hug that filled every inch of him with joy. But the feeling was more than mere contentedness. It was like placing the last piece of a jigsaw puzzle onto the board, or finishing a work of art, or stepping through one's own front door after a long day. He felt complete.

"I do have a couple of questions, actually," said Taylor, as he finally drew back from Satomi. "Is Vice Provost Adra dead?"

Casey answered that question. "While I was piloting away from the Nexus, I monitored a bunch of launches, Cap," she said. "It's possible that her Destroyer could have been one of them. But the explosion put out a ton of radiation, making the sensors pretty much useless at the moment."

"I slammed that maniac steel-skin into the wall harder than a wreckin' ball, Cap," said Blake, "Ain't no way she got up from that."

Taylor nodded. He didn't want to question Blake, but Adra was as tough as anyone he'd ever come across, and he didn't want to discount the possibility she had survived, and escaped.

"What was your second question?" asked Satomi, with interest.

"The second one is a question for each of you, actually," said Taylor, becoming suddenly more earnest. "It's the same question, but you each have to answer individually, and honestly." The others all fidgeted uncomfortably, but then waited for Taylor to continue. "We've destroyed the Nexus, which means that every simulant in the galaxy will be going offline or is already defunct," Taylor resumed. "We've given Sonner and Earth Fleet their best chance to win the war, and maybe, who knows, we've even helped the Hedalt break some chains too." Then he looked at each of them in turn: Blake, Casey and finally Satomi. "And we've put our crew back together. Our family."

"What are you asking, Cap?" said Casey.

"We don't owe Earth Fleet a thing more. We've

done enough, already," said Taylor. "We could take this ship and go wherever we want, together. We don't need to risk our necks fighting Earth's last war. So my question is, what do you all want to do next? Do we jump to Earth and join the fight, or pick a star and find our own path?"

Blake was quick to answer, "I ain't runnin' from a fight, Cap," he said gruffly, "Sonner helped save me and the rest of us. We ain't square 'til we've kicked those bastards off Earth."

Taylor nodded and then looked at Casey, who smiled and hooked her arm through Blake's, "The stars aren't going anywhere, Cap. Let's finish this first, and then I'll fly us anywhere you want."

Taylor found himself smiling again. Finally, he turned to Satomi. "And what about you? You've only been back maybe an hour or so, are you ready to put your life on the line so soon?"

"I may have only been back in this body for a short time, but I've been with you all along, Taylor," replied Satomi. "This is my journey, just as much as yours. Earth may not be our planet or our home, not really, but it doesn't matter. We were all there at the start of this and we all need to see it through to the end."

"Okay then," said Taylor taking a pace back so he was standing in front his full crew once again. In many ways, they were the same people he knew from his memories, but they were also different and unique, just as he was. And each of them was a part of the other. He hadn't realized how much he needed them until that moment, when they were finally all back together.

"Casey, set a course for Earth," said Taylor.

"Aye aye, Captain Taylor Ray..."

TWENTY-THREE

The crew of Nimrod Command were as silent as deep space as the bright blue orb shone back at them, magnified on the ship's viewport. Even Colonel Collins, who was sitting in the command chair with Sarah Sonner by his side, didn't ruin the spectacle by trying to talk it away with a grandiose speech, or spoil the moment by opening his mouth at all.

To Sonner, Earth looked exactly the same as she remembered it. Despite more than three centuries having elapsed since the fall of their world, from her perspective it hadn't been all that long since she had last looked out on the beautiful blue planet. Her last view of Earth had been when blasting out of the High Haven orbital space port as the Hedalt armada pummeled it with hundreds of plasma shards. She remembered looking back at the planet then and wondering if she'd ever see it again, before the ship she was on made the first of many chaotic jumps to secret rendezvous points, eventually arriving at the Contingency base more than a year later. But the thrill at seeing Earth again soon vanished as scan reports came in and the size of the Hedalt armada became clear.

"Technical Specialist Sonner, do you have an exact readout on the strength of the enemy forces?" Sonner asked her brother, as more of the seventy-eight remaining Nimrod-class cruisers blinked into space around them. They had left the transports, which were carrying the non-combat personnel, at the last blind jump point, where they would be safe. Though Sonner couldn't shake dark thoughts of what their eventual fate would be if the assault on Earth failed and they were left stranded in space, alone and defenseless.

"Reading twenty-five squadrons, Commander," James replied from the mission ops console, "That's one hundred twenty-five enemy ships in total. Seventy-five register as heavy cruisers or frigate-class warships."

Shit... Sonner thought. She was the first to admit she was no military strategist, but from experience she knew it would take twice their numbers just to tackle the heavy cruisers alone. She steeled herself, ready to confront Collins, but he spoke first, before she got the chance.

"Order the fleet to form up," said Collins, "Execute attack pattern Nimrod Alpha Four, as per the plan."

There were nervous replies of 'yes Colonel' from all stations and then the fleet began to organize itself, squadron by squadron, in front of Nimrod Command. Sonner could already see gaps in the formation, because many units were already below full strength after the assault on the base.

"Colonel, we have to adjust our strategy," said Sonner, trying to keep her voice low and level so that she couldn't be overheard by the other crew. "A squadron-by-squadron direct attack isn't going to work. They know we're coming and each of their squadrons outguns ours."

"We have to stick to the plan, Commander," said Collins, shifting uncomfortably, "there's no time for anything else."

"Colonel, the original plan relied on a surprise attack against a smaller force and against ships broadly comparable to our own," Sonner argued, struggling to keep emotion out of her voice. "We have none of those advantages. A direct assault won't work."

"Enough, Commander!" snapped Collins, and though he had not intended to shout, his voice carried clearly to the other stations. Anxious eyes glanced back towards them, before the crew again snapped their heads forward as Collins glared back. The Colonel waited until he felt that the others were no longer listening and glowered up at Sonner. The volume of his voice was lower, but his tone was no less severe. "Once their losses mount up, they will fracture and run," Collins seethed. "It is just one planet to them. They will not sacrifice their lives for just one world, knowing that we will fight to the last."

"The Nimrod Fleet has reported in, Colonel," interrupted James, "We're in position."

"Full attack, Mr. Sonner," said Collins, before looking back at the young officer's sister, "You will see soon enough, Commander," he said with an arrogance so thick Sonner could almost taste it in the air. "We will break their spirit."

Sonner shook her head. There was no point arguing now; the order had been given, and all she could do was hope that she was wrong. But she also knew that hope was a worthless strategy. Collins had never faced the Hedalt of Warfare Command, while Sonner had. She knew they would never break, never retreat and never stop, until every last one of their ships had been destroyed. "You're a fool, Colonel," she said. "A fool who will lead humanity to its end."

"You are relieved from duty, Commander Sonner," replied Collins, keeping control of his temper. "Return to your quarters."

"You can go to hell, Colonel," Sonner hit back, "which is where you're about to send us all."

Collins rose from his chair, and went to grab Sonner in order to forcibly remove her from the bridge, but Sonner smacked away his hand and squared off against him.

"I'm not going anywhere, Colonel."

Collins froze, flooded with anger, yet also stumped for a way to respond to Sonner's brazen challenge. But the standoff didn't have chance to escalate, as James' voice cut through the silence and drew their focus back to the mission.

"Sir, the vanguard has engaged the Hedalt," he called out; his face had suddenly drained of blood. He read the report, blurting the words out in a panic. "Three full squadrons destroyed... The others have broken off... Heavy damage to ten more ships... Casualty reports are coming in..."

"Damn it, pull them back!" cried Sonner, "A frontal assault is suicide! We must split up their forces, lure them into the asteroid belt if we can. Avoid the frigates and focus our attacks where they are weakest. Whittle down their numbers – hit and run!"

"No!" cried Collins, "That is not the plan!"

"Damn you, Colonel, the plan will get us all killed! Wake up before we're all dead!"

The mission ops console bleeped an angry alert and James checked it, hands shaking, "Five Hedalt squadrons have pushed through, led by War Frigates..." he began, "Seven more Nimrods destroyed. Ten Hedalt damaged, and only three destroyed. Colonel, what do we do?!"

Collins didn't answer directly and instead continued to babble, "We follow the plan! It will work, it must work!" His own face had also drained of blood, which combined with his bony features and white hair gave him the ghostly appearance of death incarnate.

"Hedalt cruisers on an intercept course!" called out the officer from the tactical station.

Sonner looked to Collins, but he was trapped in a trance-like state, babbling and rubbing his knuckles frantically. "Colonel!" Sonner shouted, grabbing his shoulders, "Colonel!" But there was no answer. Sonner growled and dragged Collins away from the command chair, before turning to face the front of the bridge. Both the pilot and the Tactical Specialist were looking to her, faces full of fear. "Don't just sit there, take evasive action!" Sonner called out, "Return fire, target their bridge and engines. If we can't destroy them, let's at least make sure they can't destroy us!"

"Aye Commander!" came the reply from the two stations.

Nimrod Command began to veer away from the oncoming ships, but then an explosion rippled through the deck plating across the rear of the bridge, filling the air with a pale, metallic-tasting smoke. Sonner was thrust forward by the blast and only managed to avoid smashing face-first into the deck by instinctively grasping onto the command chair.

"Pilot, pulse the main ion engines!" Sonner called out, "Put some distance between us and those ships!" She knew that a sudden burst from their powerful main engines risked accelerating them directly into another ship, but if they stayed where they were, she also knew they'd be dead in seconds. She felt the kick of the engines, and then clawed herself upright using the back of the command chair. "Damage report!" she cried out, barking harsh coughs as the acrid smoke entered her lungs.

"Direct hit..." James called back, "Hull breach aft, sections three and four. Jump systems offline."

Sonner glanced aft to where the explosion had occurred and saw Collins lying face up, eyes open, with three large shards of fractured deck plating embedded into his side and neck. Sonner cursed, *Damn you, Colonel, you don't deserve to die early! You should have lived long enough to see what you've done!*

She tried to put Collins out of her mind. Pumps whirred, clearing the dust and smoke as Sonner dropped into the command chair and checked the tactical readout. Their fleet was already down to forty-seven Nimrods, while the Hedalt armada was still over one hundred strong. A dozen possible courses of action raced through her mind, but there was only one that would ensure their survival, at least for a time. They had to run. But first, they had to regroup and get themselves out of the hornet's nest they had willingly flown into.

"Technical Specialist Sonner, open a channel, fleet wide," Sonner called out. James worked fast and a few seconds later her younger brother looked towards the command chair and nodded. Sonner took a deep breath and then spoke, hoping that her voice would sound strong and free of fear. "Nimrod Fleet, this is Commander Sarah Sonner. Colonel Collins is dead; I am taking command of the fleet." The other officers on the bridge again shot each other shaky glances, but this time a glimmer of hope also flickered behind their eyes. Sonner hurriedly entered a series of commands into the console in her chair and then sent the message fleet wide, "I'm sending new orders now. All squadrons are to fall back and re-group at the designated co-ordinates. Compute jump to escape point alpha, immediately."

"Commander, our jump systems are still down," said the pilot.

"Compute the jump; we'll get the engines back online," said Sonner, convincingly, though she had no idea how severe the damage was. The pilot nodded and turned back.

"Fleet responding," said James, and then he hesitated, "... wait, we have a problem."

"Just one?" said Sonner, cocking her head towards her brother.

"The Hedalt seem to have been targeting the fleet's jump systems deliberately," James went on, oblivious to Sonner's gallows humor, "They've knocked out the jump capabilities of more than half the fleet. No... wait, it's worse. More than eighty percent of the fleet can't jump!"

Sonner balled her hands into fists and pressed her eyes shut as dark thoughts penetrated her mind. *More than three centuries of waiting, only to fail now. It would have been better to have died in my stasis chamber with the others. At least then I wouldn't have felt hope. I wouldn't have felt anything at all...* "Has the fleet re-grouped at the fallback point?" said Sonner, still with her eyes shut.

"Yes," James answered, "But, Sarah, we can't escape. What do we do?"

Sonner opened her eyes and looked at James, then met the eyes of the ship's pilot and tactical officer. "We do what we came here to do," she said, realizing that there was no other option now, "We fight." Then she pointed to the pilot, "You, what's your name?"

"Choudary, sir," the pilot said. "Kir Choudary."

Sonner looked across to the tactical console,

"And you?"

"Melinda Suarez, Commander."

"I'm not going to lie to you, Kir Choudary and Melinda Suarez," said Sonner, "I don't know if we have a chance in hell of beating this armada. But, I do know those smug bastards think we can't win. How about we prove them wrong?"

Smiles flickered on each of their lips. They glanced at each other and nodded, before turning back to their stations.

The mission ops console sounded another angry alert and Sonner sighed, "What is it now?"

"Checking..." answered James, "It's a jump signature! Another ship just entered the system. It's... oh no..."

"What do you mean, 'oh no'?" said Sonner, throwing her hands up in despair.

"It's the capital ship from the attack on the base," said James, putting the image of the giant War Carrier on the viewport. They all watched as the other Hedalt squadrons formed up behind the hulking new mass, creating a wall of firepower that could have obliterated a small moon, never mind the rag-tag remains of the Nimrod Fleet.

Sonner pushed herself off the chair, mouth dry and heart racing, "Oh hell, no..."

TWENTY-FOUR

Sonner glanced down at the tactical readout on her chair's console; forty-two Nimrods had made it to the rendezvous. She guessed that the War Carrier alone could probably destroy half that number, but for some reason the Hedalt armada was still holding formation, and advancing so sedately that they almost appeared non-threatening. But then she heard the familiar chime on an incoming message, and she understood why they hadn't yet been obliterated. The Hedalt commander wanted the humans to know they were beaten first. They wanted to see the fear in their eyes. Have them beg for mercy, perhaps. Sonner would not give them the satisfaction.

"It's the capital ship, Commander," announced James, "they want to speak to whoever is in command."

Sonner glanced back at the broken body of Colonel Collins. *Off the hook again, Colonel...* she thought to herself, before turning to face the viewport. She adjusted her uniform, brushing dust and flecks of debris off her shoulders, and then straightened her back, rising to her full height. "Put them on the viewport..."

The viewport switched to an image of a Hedalt soldier. To Sonner's surprise, it was not Provost Adra, but someone new. The soldier had slicked back hair that seemed to give off a sheen like polished copper and looked similarly inflexible. His armored uniform had a striking amber lining and he was powerfully built, even for a Hedalt soldier. Two other soldiers flanked him, in similar armored units, and surrounding them all was an expansive, high-tech bridge, populated by dozens of simulants, each moving from station to station, performing the duties necessary to operate such a titanic vessel.

"I am High Provost Kagan," said the soldier, whose melodious voice did not match his stern appearance. "Tell me your name, commander of the human fleet."

"Something tells me you don't really care what my name is," Sonner answered, snarkily. She had thought that Adra was the most obnoxious Hedalt she was ever likely to meet, but she had a feeling that this new High Provost was going to claim Adra's crown. "Now if you wouldn't mind getting out of our way, you're blocking the route to Earth. You know, our home planet? The one you stole?"

Kagan's eyes narrowed just a fraction, but enough to let Sonner know that she had already gotten under his skin. "How little you know of your own world," replied Kagan, his lyrical voice conveying his palpable disdain. "But it does not matter. Soon humanity will finally be extinct. I was merely curious to see who had led your species in such a foolish attack. That you ever considered yourselves a match for the Hedalt Empire amuses me greatly."

"You must be a blast at parties," quipped Sonner, but the remark was obviously lost on the High Provost. "This isn't over yet."

Kagan snorted a laugh, "I admire your spirit, human, if nothing else," he sneered. "I was hoping to find the rogue simulants among you, but it seems their allegiance to your cause was short-lived after all. A pity, but I will find them soon enough; it is only a matter of time."

Though he didn't comprehend it, Kagan had inadvertently buoyed Sonner's confidence. Until that moment, Sonner had no way of knowing whether Taylor's mission had succeeded or failed, or even if he was still alive at all. But if Kagan had yet to locate them, there was still hope. Maybe only a glimmer, but still enough to cling to. *Come on Taylor...* Sonner thought, *we need your party trick now more than ever...*

"All squadrons, target what is left of the pitiful human fleet," Kagan called out, to a crew member or simulant out of sight of the image on the viewport. "But leave the lead ship untouched. I want them to see their friends burn in the cold void of space, before I personally board their ship and execute them.

"You know where to find me, Kagan," snarled Sonner, and then she turned to James, ready to give the order for the fleet to attack, but suddenly Kagan's image on the viewport crackled and distorted, and their own systems flickered and glitched at the same time, before returning to normal.

"What was that?" said Sonner, looking to James to provide an explanation. But her brother didn't need to offer an answer. Instead, he just pointed to the viewport and smiled. Sonner frowned and stared back at the image of High Provost Kagan. The bridge of his massive ship was in chaos. All the simulants were jerking and spasming violently, as if they'd been struck by lightning or were being controlled by a sadistic puppeteer. Some collapsed onto their consoles, some exploded as if a grenade had gone off inside their chests, while others just fell down and lay motionless, stiff as a board.

"He did it!" James cried. "Taylor and the others, they must have taken down the Nexus!"

Sonner punched a quick command into her console and brought up an external view of the approaching armada in one half of the viewport, leaving the bridge of Kagan's ship on the other half. She laughed out loud as the Hedalt warships began to veer out of formation, thrusters and engines malfunctioning randomly. At least a dozen ships had already swerved into others, and explosions were popping off throughout the Hedalt armada, like fireworks. Sonner looked back at the High Provost but he was twisting and turning in all directions, barking orders and demanding to know what was going on. Sonner decided that it was only fair she should clue him in.

"I'm afraid we'll have to decline your gracious offer of extermination today, High Provost," she said, feeling a rush of adrenaline surge through her body like nothing she'd experienced before. "Oh, and you might want to find yourself some new crew members."

"What have you done?!" barked Kagan, his voice raw and bereft of its musical timbres.

"Those rogue simulants you were asking about earlier?" Sonner delighted in explaining herself to Kagan. "Well, they just destroyed your precious Nexus. Sorry about that..."

"Impossible!" Kagan snarled, "You lie!"

"Believe whatever you like, Hedalt," Sonner hit back. The elation of their sudden reprieve was now hardening into a steely resolve to finish what they had come here to do. She turned her head fractionally towards James and said, "Tell the fleet to attack. Clear out the smaller ships first – the ones with the fewest simulants – and then take out the cruisers."

"You will not succeed!" Kagan blared.

"Watch me..." said Sonner, with the bite of a king cobra. Then she sat down in the command chair and crossed her legs, casually. "Oh, and leave the lead ship untouched," she added to her brother, raising the point of a finger as if she'd just remembered something important, "I want the High Provost to watch his armada crumble, before I personally board his ship and take it as a prize."

Kagan roared, sending strands of his perfectly slicked-back brown hair tumbling across his face like oily tentacles. But as satisfying as it was to watch Kagan break down, Sonner had already seen enough of his face. She cut the connection with a single command on her console.

"Choudary, Suarez, target their jump engines. Make sure that capital can't leave," Sonner called out to an ecstatic chorus of "Aye Commander!" in reply. Turning to James, she added, "Get Echo Squadron to form up on us. And tell them to suit up for a boarding raid."

"Aye Commander," James called back, before punching the commands into his console with renewed vigor. "Echo Squadron is responding, but we've got another problem – a second jump signature..." but then he turned to her and smiled, "It's the Contingency One!"

Sonner beamed back at the him. "Put them on the viewport!"

James entered the command and instantly the simulant form of Taylor appeared on the viewport.

"Hey Commander, did we miss all the fun?" said Taylor, sitting in the command chair as if it were just another regular day at the office.

"Your party trick came in the nick of time, Captain," Sonner replied, "But, no, the fun's just getting started."

"Sorry for the delay, Commander," said Satomi, appearing at Taylor's side and resting a hand on his shoulder. "The ripple effect from the destruction of the Nexus may travel at super-luminal speeds, but Earth is still some distance from the Hedalt home world."

Sonner's eyebrows almost reached her hairline. She looked at Taylor, while jabbing a finger in the direction of Satomi. "Is this?..."

"Yes, it is," Taylor answered, unable to contain his delight. "Commander Sarah Sonner, meet Satomi Rose."

"I look forward to meeting you in person,

Satomi Rose," said Sonner brightly, "I suggest we all get together later. On Earth."

"Aye aye, Commander Sarah Sonner," replied Taylor, throwing up a casual salute. Sonner heard Casey in the background calling out, "Stop stealing my lines!"

"Commander, we have another inbound jump signature," interrupted James, "It's a single Hedalt ship. Destroyer class."

"A friend of yours, Captain?" Sonner asked.

Taylor checked the sensor readings on his console, "A mutual friend of ours, I'm afraid..." he replied, gravely.

"Not for much longer. James, add the Destroyer to the target list, and have Charlie Squadron take it down, top priority,"

"Hold that order, James," Taylor called out, "If you don't mind Commander, this one is ours."

Sonner smiled and nodded, "I understand, Captain. She's all yours."

"Thank you, Sarah," said Taylor, "When you're done up here, let us know where to meet. And, you're buying."

"Well, since you can't drink, I'll buy your crew as many rounds as you like!" laughed Sonner. Then with genuine warmth she added, "I'll see you soon, Taylor." Then she switched the viewport to show the Hedalt capital ship in a window to the side. Fires were seeping out into space from where

Suarez had drilled into its massive hull with turret fire, taking out its jump systems with clinical precision. Sonner smiled back at Taylor, "But first, I'm planning a little ship upgrade..."

TWENTY-FIVE

Kir Choudary piloted the Nimrod-class cruiser beneath the vast underbelly of Kagan's War Carrier and towards the large rear docking bay doors. The difference in scale between the two ships was even more startling up close, so much so that the capital ship had blocked out the light from the sun and cast them into shadow. That their advance had gone completely unchallenged, without even a warning message from Kagan, made the approach feel eerie, as if they were about to board a ghost ship. But while the simulant crew may have been disabled, Sonner knew that there were still soldiers on board that were very much alive, and who would not go down without a fight.

Some of the other smaller Hedalt battleships had limped on and mounted a spirited resistance, but these had been quickly overcome by the freshly reinvigorated Nimrod Fleet. And with only one or, at most, two Hedalt soldiers on board, the larger cruisers were effectively crippled without their simulant crews. Some sporadically fired back at the fleet, but it was like fighting with only one leg and an arm tied behind their back, making it easy for the agile Nimrods to evade their cannons and pick them off.

Choudary completed his approach and enabled the mag-locks, clamping the Nimrod to the docking bay doors like a limpet on a whale.

"Hard dock confirmed, Commander Sonner," announced Choudary as the solid thump of metal connecting with metal resounded through the ship's frame. "Suarez is cutting through now."

"Is Echo Squadron in position?" asked Sonner.

"Affirmative, Commander, the five Nimrods from Echo are docked and sealed, awaiting your instructions."

Sonner pushed herself out of the command chair. She had already donned her body armor and had a sidearm strapped to her hip. Eighteen in total would board the capital ship in an effort to seize control from Kagan. Sonner had seen three Hedalt on the bridge, and it was possible there were more, but knowing how heavily they relied on simulants, she doubted it. For all she cared, the rest of the Hedalt fleet could burn in space, but this ship she intended to take as a prize. This wasn't out of a desire for revenge or for reasons of pride, but for the future defense of Earth. With the simulants gone, she did not expect Warfare Command would mount another attack any time soon, even if they were capable of doing so. But, just in case the Hedalt decided to come knocking again, she would need a way to repel the threat. And what better way than to turn the Hedalt's most powerful weapon against them.

"The bridge is yours, Mr. Choudary," said Sonner, heading towards the central corridor that lead to the docking hatch. "Please don't leave without us..."

Sonner heard spirited Choudary's reply, but she was already bustling along the corridor towards the airlock, where Suarez and James were waiting.

"We're ready to breach, Commander," said Suarez, "the boarding parties from Echo are standing by too."

Sonner drew her weapon and loaded it, "I hate these damn things," she grumbled. "I hope you're a better shot with one of these than me, Suarez."

"Yes, Commander, I'm the best," replied Suarez, without even a hint of boastfulness. Sonner wasn't sure if this was just arrogance or egotism, neither of which she was a fan of, but hearing Suarez's calmly self-assured reply actually made her feel better.

"Okay, let's go and steal ourselves a new ship," Sonner continued, "Breach in three... two... one..."

Suarez hit the hatch release, which swung open like the lid of a jack-in-the-box. Air rushed past their faces and then Suarez charged through first, followed by James and then Sonner. They had expected a volley of plasma to greet them, but they were met only with silence as they entered into what looked like a fighter bay.

"Clear!" Suarez called out using one of the dozen or more smaller ships for cover. Then similar calls of 'Clear' were heard from other parts of the deck as Echo breached and also took up defensive positions inside the bay.

Sonner stepped up to one of the smaller craft and inspected it. Each was armed with plasma cannons on the ends of their sleek wing tips and what looked like a smaller turret on the nose.

"These are fighter craft," said Suarez, pulling herself up to peer inside the cockpit of the closest ship. "Single seater. There's a defunct simulant inside this one."

"Looks like we're going to need to train some fighter pilots then," said Sonner, running a hand along the hull of the agile-looking vessel, as the breaching teams from Echo Squadron moved up and took positions further inside the hangar.

"You've got one volunteer, Commander," said Suarez, eying up the fighter as if it were a brand new supercar in a showroom.

"If we manage to take over this ship, you've got yourself a deal, Miss Suarez," said Sonner. "Let's go..."

They moved cautiously through the cavernous interior of the War Carrier, checking section by section for signs of ambush or resistance, but all they found were the non-functional bodies of simulant crew. Eventually, they climbed up a long, elegant stairway, of the sort that wouldn't have looked out of place on a twentieth-century luxury ocean liner, to reach a wide set of doors.

"Just through there is the bridge, as best as I can make out," said James, referring to their limited scan data of the ship on a data pad.

"As best as you can make out?" replied Sonner, raising her eyebrows at him. "I need you to do better than that, mister."

"Sorry, Commander," James answered, "More than eighty percent of this ship is given over to weapons systems and that fighter bay we walked into. The rest, I'm just guessing at. But I'm pretty sure this is the bridge."

"Well, I guess 'pretty sure' will have to do," said Sonner, shrugging. It wasn't like she was about to turn back. "Suarez, you're up..."

Suarez nodded and signaled the other teams from Echo, before counting down from five using hand signals alone. Sonner took a deep breath and raised her weapon. *Here goes nothing...*

The door swung open and Suarez burst inside along with the first team from Echo Squadron, but in contrast to the deathly calm throughout the rest of the ship, this time the enemy were waiting.

Plasma shards flashed towards them and Suarez immediately fired back, hitting one of the Hedalt soldiers in the neck, while a second soldier in amber-lined armor was battered by a hail of bullets from the first Echo team. But neither of the soldiers was Kagan.

Sonner and James followed, but they'd barely made it across the threshold before the doors slammed shut behind them, trapping one of the Echo team members and crushing him like a bug. Both Sonners were frozen with shock, unable to tear their eyes away from the gruesome scene. But as grisly as it was, the fact that the bulk of their raiding party was now trapped outside was even harder to stomach. Sonner cursed. They'd just lost their advantage of numbers.

Kagan sprang up from behind a row of consoles and unleashed a storm of plasma from pistols held in both hands, lighting up the bridge like a laser show.

"Move!" cried Suarez, charging towards the shell-shocked duo and knocking Sonner to the deck just as a shard of plasma clipped James' shoulder. He dropped, yelling as the searing pain took hold, but managed to scramble behind a console alongside Suarez and Sonner. More flashes of plasma seared the air, scorching the deck to their side and burning holes in the wall behind them as Kagan continued to unload.

Sonner glanced across to where the team from Echo had entered, but they all lay dead, hit multiple times in the head and upper body. The Earth Fleet body armor had proved no match for the weapons Kagan was wielding.

"Did you really think you could take my ship, human?" shouted Kagan, his voice echoing around the bridge. "With or without simulants, I will destroy you! Others will come. It is only a matter of time."

"Big talk, considering your fleet is in ashes," Sonner called back. "And this is my ship now, so I'd appreciate it if you stopped shooting it up."

James looked at her, mouth agape, "What are you doing?" he asked in a panicked whisper.

"I'm trying to make him angry, make him slip up," said Sonner.

"I think he's already angry!"

More shards of plasma slammed into the console, causing a cascade of small explosions, which showered Sonner and the others with smoldering debris.

"This cover won't last for long, we have to make a move," said Sonner, "Suarez, any fancy combat tactics you can offer?"

"Nothing fancy, Commander," Suarez replied, brushing a burning ember from her hair. "But how about I run out to the side and draw his fire, while you move right and take him down."

"You're the crack shot," said Sonner, flinching as the panel to the side of her head burst open and crackled with electrical energy, "I should be the one to draw his fire."

James shook his head, "No, let me, the fleet can't lose its Commander."

"James, this is no time for heroics..." Sonner began, but James was resolute.

"No heroics, Sarah, it's just common sense," he said, "I'll go, and you two take that bastard down."

The console began to crumble and a shard of plasma ripped through, barely a meter to their side. "Okay, but if you get..."

"I won't, Sarah, just make sure you get him!" Then James rose to a crouch, "Ready?" Sonner and Suarez nodded and raised their weapons, and as another shower of debris lashed his face, James ran, firing wildly in the direction of High Provost Kagan.

Suarez was up first, but her eyes widened as it become obvious that Kagan hadn't taken the bait. Instead of switching his aim to James, he had anticipated the move and was aiming dead at her. Plasma flashed from the barrel as Suarez tried desperately to dodge, but the shard raked across her body armor, gouging out a furrow of material and flesh. Suarez screamed as Sonner fired, but Kagan had already moved, darting towards James so fast he was almost a blur.

James slid to a stop, realizing that their plan had failed, and fired at Kagan, but the round pinged off his amber-edged armor like a hailstone off a car hood. Before he knew what was happening, Kagan had discarded one of the plasma pistols and had grabbed him by the neck, lifting him so that his toes were barely scraping on the deck.

"Put him down!" Sonner yelled, stepping out from behind the burning mass of metal that had been their cover, keeping the barrel of her weapon aimed at Kagan. "Do it now, or I will kill you!"

Kagan laughed, and swung the flailing body of James in front of him so that he hung between himself and Sonner like a shield. She could hear his pained gurgles and croaks as Kagan slowly squeezed the life out of him, "Take your shot, human. If you dare!"

Damn it! Sonner cursed, keeping the weapon trained on the small gap to the side of her brother's thrashing arms and legs. She knew she would as likely hit him as Kagan, but if she didn't shoot, he'd be dead anyway, with herself following soon after. Kagan knew this. He wanted her to shoot. He wanted her to kill him, to give him some sick sense of satisfaction. She added pressure to the trigger, but she couldn't do it. She couldn't risk killing her brother.

In front of her, she heard Kagan's long, melodious laugh again, "Pathetic, weak-minded human! And you wonder why we sought to exterminate you..."

A loud crack punctured the air and Sonner flinched, instinctively checking herself, but she was unhurt. She turned and saw Suarez, propped up behind the broken console, barely visible through the smoke and twisted material. She was clutching her wounded side with one hand, while in the other was her weapon, smoke oozing from the barrel, which was aimed dead at Kagan. Sonner spun again and saw her brother desperately scrambling away from the High Provost, who had sunk to his knees, clutching his neck with both hands where Suarez's bullet had ruptured the flesh. Kagan's remaining weapon lay discarded on the deck beside him.

Sonner ran over to James and dropped down by his side.

"I'm okay..." James croaked, grabbing her arm with one hand, while still holding his bruised neck with the other.

Sonner rose, and stepped in front of Kagan, kicking the plasma pistol clear of his reach. He looked up at her with hateful eyes. Even now as he drowned in his own blood, Sonner could not understand his vehement contempt for her and the human race. He tried to speak, but all that came out of his mouth was blood. She considered shooting him, but there had already been enough death and violence. And in some twisted way, she imagined that Kagan would probably consider her act of 'mercy' as an insult. Kagan spluttered again, staining the amber lining of his armor with a streak of bright red blood. Then he fell forward and lay in a slowly expanding pool of his own blood, squirming for a few moments more, before finally falling still.

Sonner heard boots shuffling across the deck and turned to see Melinda Suarez hobbling up beside her. She saw the scorched wound and then grasped the tactical specialist by the shoulders, worried she was about to collapse. Suarez gladly accepted Sonner's help, resting an arm over her shoulder for support.

"We need to get that wound seen to," said Sonner, "We've lost enough people already. And there weren't many of us to begin with."

"I'm not dying today, Commander," said Suarez, and Sonner was amazed to see that the outline of a smile managed to crack through her pained grimace.

"And why is that, Tactical Specialist Melinda Suarez?" Sonner replied, as the doors to the bridge burst open and the other Echo teams raced inside, carrying an assortment of tools and equipment. One of them saw Suarez and rushed to her side, medkit in hand.

"Because I'm going to be a fighter pilot," said Suarez, grinning, as Sonner helped to lay her down on the deck so that the medic could attend to her.

"Well, a deal is a deal, I guess," laughed Sonner, backing away to give the medic space. "You were certainly right about one thing, though."

"What's that, Commander?" Suarez groaned as the medic began to peel away the charred armor surrounding the wound.

"You are the best damn shot in the fleet."

TWENTY-SIX

The lone Destroyer that jumped in did not join the battle, as Taylor had expected. Instead, it was headed on a direct course for Earth. Casey had managed to shunt enough power to the main ion engines to catch up with it, but despite repeated attempts to contact the vessel and warn it off, the Destroyer had not responded.

"What's our time to intercept?" asked Taylor, perched on the edge of the command chair.

"We'll catch it before it hits atmosphere, Cap," said Casey. "Less than a minute."

"Try and raise it again," said Taylor, glancing across to Satomi at mission ops. "Tell them to stand down or we will open fire."

"Message sent, Captain," replied Satomi, "but since they didn't listen the first four times, I don't expect they'll listen now."

Flashes of plasma erupted from the rear turret of the Destroyer, but Casey managed to weave between them.

"Damn, that was close," said Blake, "I'm glad you're still awake over there, Casey." Casey threw up a casual salute, but kept her eyes fixed inside the pilot's viewport.

"I think that's your answer, Captain," said Satomi, "the choice is to let them land, or not."

"But they're a sitting duck," said Taylor, gesturing to the ship on the viewport, which had not attempted any evasive maneuvers since their pursuit had begun, "It somehow doesn't seem right to shoot it down."

"Cap, we're talkin' 'bout the guys who nearly wiped out all life on Earth," replied Blake, shooting him a reproving look, "I think we're *way* past playin' fair."

"Fair point," said Taylor. It was hard to argue, though he still didn't like the idea of shooting someone in the back, even if that someone was Vice Provost Adra. "See if you can take out their main engines, that will at least buy us time to figure out our next move."

"The ship's momentum will still carry it into the atmosphere, even if you disable the engines," Satomi pointed out. "The difference is that without the main engines it won't be able to slow down before it gets there."

"Well, if nothing else, it should motivate them to answer our damn calls," Taylor replied, "unless Adra wants to get cooked in the atmosphere, that is." Then he turned to the tactical station and added, "Do it, Blake."

"You got it, Cap," said Blake, swiftly targeting the Destroyer's main ion drives, "One disabled Hedalt ship, comin' right up." A burst of turret fire rippled out ahead of them and lashed across the rear of the Destroyer, causing a succession of micro explosions. A few seconds later, the bright glow from the engine exhausts flickered and went out. Blake spun around in his chair and grinned, "Am I good, or what?"

Suddenly, an intense flash of light saturated the viewport as the Destroyer exploded violently, breaking apart into a dozen fiery hulks that shot out in all directions. Casey reacted with the reflexes of a cat, narrowly avoiding a collision with one of the larger fragments.

"Blake, I said disable it, not obliterate it!" cried Taylor.

"Hey, I barely tickled the thing," said Blake, leaping on the defensive, "There's no way I hit it hard enough to make it pop like that!"

"He's right, Captain," said Satomi, peering intently into her console screen, "I'm picking up what looks like an escape shuttle pushing ahead of the debris." She punched in a few commands and the image on the viewport shifted to show a small v-shaped craft that was only big enough for one or two people, at a squeeze.

Taylor noticed there were electrical arcs spiking all over the rear section, "It looks like it's damaged."

"Some debris might have collided with the shuttle after it ejected," suggested Satomi. "My guess is that they were hoping to mask their escape with the explosion, and then slip away in the confusion. And it almost worked."

"Can we scoop it up into the cargo hold?" asked Taylor.

"Not before it reaches atmosphere," said Casey, "I'm going to have to slow down too, otherwise all that will be left of us and this ship is what they can scrape off the surface of Earth."

"Damn it! Okay, monitor the shuttle and follow it down," said Taylor, "I guess we're going to have to meet with our provost friend one last time."

TWENTY-SEVEN

Casey followed the escape shuttle into the cloud-covered, blue atmosphere of Earth. The smaller ship's higher entry speed opened up a gap between them, and as the Contingency One finally emerged from the flames and into the upper atmosphere, the escape shuttle was already several hundred miles ahead.

"It's going down fast, Captain," said Satomi, "Probably too fast..."

"Can you project where it will land?" asked Taylor, scanning the horizon as they approached lower over what should have been the western United States, though he didn't recognize it. "I know that technically I've never been to this planet before, but if the original Taylor's memories are true, this should be California, right?"

"That's right, we're heading towards what should be the ruins of San Francisco, but there's no trace of the city at all, or any of its suburbs," said Satomi, "The escape shuttle has crashed into the sand dunes around what was Golden Gate Park."

"Sand dunes, what the hell?" said Blake. "Are you sure this is Earth?"

"There's no question it's Earth," said Satomi, "The continents are all exactly where they should be, but comparing the geographical records in the archives to what the planet looks like now... well, it's quite a transformation."

"Transformed how?" asked Taylor, as they descended lower. "We should be able to see the bridge by now, but it's like it's not there."

"That's because it isn't," said Satomi. "It's almost as if the whole area has been sent back in time to before the cities even existed. It'll take time to get a detailed picture of the entire planet, but from what I've seen so far, beyond some evidence of subterranean mining facilities, there are no major built up areas at all. It's almost entirely unspoilt."

"Unspoilt?" said Blake, looking and sounding completely flummoxed. "They nuked the damn planet, Satomi!"

"Don't forget that happened well over three hundred years ago, Blake," Satomi reminded him. "Background radiation levels are now below what they were even before the war, according to the fleet archives. Whatever they've been doing, and for whatever reason, the Hedalt have really cleaned the planet up."

"That makes no damn sense!" cried Blake, "Why wreck the place only to fix it again?"

Taylor shrugged, "Maybe our friend Vice Provost Adra can tell us. She owes us some answers, and I intend to get them." He looked at Casey and said, "Set us down near to where the escape shuttle landed."

"Just not too near," suggested Satomi.

"Aye aye, Technical Specialist Satomi Rose..." sang Casey, grinning back at Taylor, who just shook his head.

Although the whole bay area including the city, which was highly conspicuous by its absence, had reverted to what Taylor assumed was its natural state, there were still some structures on the surface. Around the bay and where the Golden Gate bridge would have been were a series of walkways and buildings that had been elegantly designed to blend in with the scenery. Casey set the Contingency One down on a small landing pad, which seemed to have been designed more for interplanetary shuttle craft than starships, but as usual her deftness of touch and skill meant that she could park in places most other pilots wouldn't even dream of attempting. The pad was a couple of hundred meters from where the shuttle had landed in the dunes, but other than this they had no idea where Adra had gone, or even if it had been Adra inside.

"Everyone take a weapon, just in case," said Taylor, passing them out as the rear cargo ramp lowered. "She's unlikely to welcome our arrival."

"I don't get why she came here, anyway," said Blake. "This ain't her world."

Taylor remembered back to one of his earlier confrontations with Adra, and the strange comment she'd made about Earth. "She believes that it is," he said. "She told me that once. She said Earth belonged to the Hedaltus race by right. But I never found out why."

"Well, it sure as hell ain't her world no more," Blake countered, "and to be honest, I don't feel like I know the place either."

"Let's just find her," suggested Satomi, "this won't be over while she's still out there."

They walked out of the ship and into the late afternoon sun, the salt breeze washing over them like a literal breath of fresh air compared to the staler environment of the ship's cabin. It didn't matter that they didn't breathe anymore, or that their sense of taste was as non-existent as a fifty-a-day smoker; the cool air still invigorated their minds.

They continued to move cautiously along the walkways that stretched out above the sand dunes that had replaced what would have been Golden Gate Park, along with a significant part of the modern bay area. Simulants lay scattered around the strange venue, but other than these now defunct automatons, there was not another soul in sight.

"This place is givin' me the creeps," said Blake, darting the barrel of his weapon at every shadow that flickered.

"I'll hold your hand if you like, Blakey?" teased Casey, but Blake wasn't amused.

Soon they had reached the end of one of the long walkways, which culminated in what seemed to be a viewing platform, gazing out towards Alcatraz island. Just as nothing remained of the city, there was no sign of the ancient prison either. But the viewing platform did allow Taylor to see that the escape shuttle had ditched hard into the sand, leaving a long furrow in its wake. The glass canopy of the shuttle had been ejected, but from what Taylor could see with his enhanced silver simulant eyes, there was no longer anyone inside. He could see a trail of footprints in the sand, leading over one of the taller dunes down towards the water.

"I hate the beach," grumbled Blake, still complaining, "I hope these simulant bodies are sand-proof."

"They've survived a lot worse than sand," said

Taylor, climbing over the railings and traversing the short drop down onto the dune, before waving the rest of them on.

Casey jumped down next, scowling at how the sand instantly crept inside her purple canvas shoes – her new favorites – followed by Satomi and then an increasingly grumpy Blake Meade. Taylor lead the way, following the footsteps in the sand, noticing that patches of the golden grains had been stained red. *Blood...* he thought to himself. *She's hurt.* He continued climbing, weapon held ready until he was able to peer over the peak of the sand dune. And then he saw her. Standing by the edge of the water as it gently lapped the shore was a Hedalt soldier, black armor shimmering in the warm sun like a scorpion's exoskeleton. Even from where he was standing, Taylor knew it was Adra. He could also see that she was not armed, at least not with a plasma weapon, and that she was slowly leaking blood into the sand.

Taylor clicked on the safety and put away his weapon, drawing wary glances from the others, and turned to face them. "I don't think she's here for a fight," he said, keeping his voice low, though the breeze carried his words away from the shore. "Safety your weapons, but keep them loaded, just in case I'm wrong."

"What, we're just gonna stroll over an' say 'hi'?" said Blake, reluctantly holstering his weapon.

"Yes, exactly," replied Taylor.

"Did I, or the other me you knew, ever tell you that you're outta your damn mind, Cap?" Blake protested.

"I think probably both," said Taylor, smiling. "Just follow me, but hang a little way behind. And be ready for a quick draw if it looks like she's going to kill me."

"Smooth plan, Cap," Blake went on, with obvious sarcasm, "I'm right behind ya. Waaay behind ya..."

"Thanks, Blake, I appreciate it," said Taylor with matching sarcasm, while slapping him heartily on the shoulder. Then he turned, briefly spotting the grinning faces of Satomi and Casey, before starting to make his way down the other side of the dune.

At the bottom, he gestured for the others to hang back and began walking up to Adra, careful to approach in a wide arc so that there was no possibility that the Vice Provost couldn't see him coming. The water began to lap gently against his boots, but still Adra did not respond to his approach, and as he got closer, he began to question whether this had been a wise choice after all. *Blake was right...* Taylor thought as he closed to within five meters of Adra, still without provoking a reaction. *I must be out of my mind...*

TWENTY-EIGHT

Vice Provost Adra's penetrating green eyes glanced over to Taylor, cold and severe, but then she looked out across the water, as if his sudden appearance was not unexpected.

"Have you come to gloat, simulant?" she asked, without taking her eyes away from the waves. "To revel in your triumph at handing this planet back to the parasites that tainted it?"

"I'm not here to gloat," said Taylor, sincerely. "I only want to know why you're here. The war is over. This planet doesn't belong to you anymore."

"Do you not consider yourself human?" Adra asked, ignoring his statement. Her eyes briefly flicked towards him as blood continued to flow from a deep gash in her stomach. Whatever caused the injury had been brutal enough to have split her armor.

"Part of me is human," answered Taylor, "the part you put inside this manufactured head. The part that broke free of your controls."

"But you are not one of them, simulant. I know that, because I made you." Adra was now looking at him directly. She was strangely calm, which was throwing Taylor off guard; he had expected vehement wrath or at least bitterness, but Adra displayed neither. "And you will never be one of them. For that alone, you should thank me."

Again, Adra's words mystified Taylor. *Thank her? What on Earth do I have to thank her for?* he wondered. But it did prompt perhaps the most obvious question. And it was this question, more than why she was on Earth, that was the most important. Taylor confronted her with it, "What is it about humans that you hate so much?"

Adra laughed, "I doubt you have the capability to understand, simulant."

"Try me."

Adra took a step towards Taylor and instantly Blake drew his weapon and aimed it at her. Taylor stretched out his hand and waved him off.

Adra stared back at Blake and Taylor could see a flicker of resentment in her eyes. "You cannot kill me, simulant," Adra called over to Blake. "I am already dead."

Blake glanced anxiously at Taylor, who was still

motioning for him to lower his weapon. Blake looked back at the Vice Provost and slowly dipped the barrel, but remained ready to raise it again in an instant, should she make a move.

Adra took another two paces towards Taylor so that they were no more than an arm's length apart. Despite Blake standing ready, and despite Adra's impairments, Taylor still felt vulnerable.

"The loyalty of your companions is impressive, if unexpected," said Adra, inching closer still so that they were practically face to face. "You should understand that loyalty is the only currency of worth, simulant. Do not lose it."

"I don't intend to," replied Taylor. Given the close proximity of Adra's towering figure, he was fighting a strong desire to back away.

"You asked why I hate humans. You asked why I am here," continued Adra. Her words now had more bite. "I will tell you why, simulant, so that you understand the depth of your crimes. It is the only injury I can inflict on you now. But perhaps it is enough."

If Taylor had been human, he knew that a shiver would have run down his spine at that moment. He thanked his simulant body for not revealing any emotional tells, but inside his mind he still found Adra's chilling statement deeply unsettling.

"Many thousands of Earth-centuries ago my race was taken from this planet," Adra continued, initially maintaining her piercing stare, but then she turned and gazed out towards open water again, seemingly swept up by the view.

"Your species originated on Earth?" Taylor was unsure if he'd heard her correctly, but Adra just continued to talk; she was either ignoring his question or oblivious to it.

"My ancestors were taken from this planet long ago by a race we called the Masters. The Masters had selected Earth as a testing ground for a biological experiment. It is not known exactly when..." Then Adra again glanced at Taylor, but this time the bitterness oozed out like the blood from her wound, "...and were it not for you, I would be here now, uncovering those secrets." Then her eyes softened slightly and she looked back across the water, as if her temporary lapse of control had never happened. "The Masters began their experiments on ancient ancestors of the verminous homo sapiens, four hundred or more thousand years before this day," Adra went on, as if she was addressing a lecture theatre of students. "The Masters had long transcended their organic form. In its place they had fabricated a more durable synthetic frame, and augmented their already superior intellect with neural implants."

Taylor chose not to interrupt again, which was helpful, because at that moment he was lost for words. It seemed clear that Adra was describing his own frame. She was describing simulant technology.

"Yet, despite their technological advantage, over the span of eons they had grown weak. With no mechanism or even urge to procreate, they continually replicated their brains to the point where the genetic degradation of their species dwindled their numbers. In time, they realized they would no longer be able operate the galactic network they had engineered, and so they needed others to do this for them. To that end they used the early hominid life forms on this planet to create a new species, splicing it with DNA from their own original organic form." Adra watched, almost transfixed as water lapped against her boots, mixing with the blood dripping from her side, before she finally broke free of the trance and continued. "For many tens of thousands more years that species was allowed to evolve on this planet. Further genetic modifications created a number of sub-species, before the Masters finally arrived at the strongest and most worthy race. The perfect race. The one that would best serve their needs. Us."

Adra's story was so compelling that Taylor had forgotten how dangerous she was. He was too swept up with wanting to know more to be concerned that Adra might still attack. "But surely there would be records of Hedalt having lived on

Earth?" Taylor asked, trying to reconcile her story, while also probing her for more details.

"Our original ancestors would not be easily recognized now," mused Adra, "The Masters continued to enhance Hedaltus DNA for many centuries after we were taken. But they are here. I intended to come to Earth to study them. To uncover more of our history." Then she suddenly grew angry again, growling, "But your meddling prevented that." Her feet shifted in the sand, as if she were about to lunge at him, and Taylor saw Blake raise his weapon in his peripheral vision. But then Adra fell heavily to one knee, teeth clenched, face contorted in immense pain.

As she dropped, Taylor caught sight of a long, black blade impaled into her chest, pressed deep into her black armor. It would have taken a powerful impact to sink the knife so deep into her flesh. *The shuttle crash...* Taylor realized.

Adra groaned and rose to her feet, cradling her chest. Taylor felt compelled to offer help. He knew the others would think him mad, but he still had his humanity, even if Adra cared nothing for their lives. "Let me get you some help," said Taylor, reaching out to her, "To treat your wound."

Adra took a pace back. "No!" she growled, "I do not want your help. I want you to finish hearing what I have to say. I want you to know what your meddling has done!"

Taylor stepped back, accepting that Adra was lost. He wasn't sure he wanted to hear what else she had to say, but like the scene of an accident, it was hard to tear his interest away.

"After the Hedaltus race was taken from this world, the Masters simply left the other genetic experiments behind," Adra began again, "They took the strongest and most worthy race, and left the failures – the genetic mistakes – behind, rather than dispose of them. In time, one of those mistakes became the homo sapiens that went on to blight this planet." Adra jabbed a blood-stained finger towards Taylor's simulant skull. "You have the memories of one of these humans. You know of their vile and treacherous lives. You know of their long and bloody history of depravity, greed, selfishness and unjust wars. And through it all this planet was made to suffer and endure their abuse. They were not worthy of Earth. We cured this planet of its sickness and returned it to its former glory. Earth belongs to the Hedaltus. It is ours by right!"

Taylor glanced back to the others, who were all listening just as intently as Taylor, their simulant ears not missing a single syllable. But it was also now apparent that Adra was dying. She had said what she wanted to say, and had nothing to lose from a desperate last attempt to crush Taylor's head. But despite the risk, Taylor still wanted to know more.

"If what you say is true, you share a history with humans," said Taylor, "Hell, you're related to them! Why not make peace. Surely that would be more worthy?"

"We are nothing like them!" Adra yelled, and Taylor could hear the metallic clank as Blake's hand grasped his weapon more tightly. But then Adra coughed blood, and she again dropped to one knee, her considerable strength finally waning. "They are insects compared to us. A pestilence. Extermination was the just recourse."

With each sentence Adra grew more enraged and more impassioned, spitting blood with each word that escaped her lips. But her eyelids were blinking more slowly now, and for a second she almost fell unconscious, but the instinctive threat of falling woke her senses. She dug her fists into the golden sand and looked up at Taylor, blood trickling from her mouth.

"And now you see your crime, simulant," Adra spat. "You have handed this planet back to the humans, for them to cast it into ruin once more." She laughed, and a line of blood ran down her chin. "And you consider *us* the enemy. You consider *us* monsters!"

Finally, Adra's strength failed to the point where she could no longer hold herself up. Drawing on her last ounce of vitality, she shuffled back in the sand and rested against the steep incline of the dune, cradling her wounded chest. She no longer looked in pain, but her steel-grey complexion had faded to a milky white. Taylor felt brave enough to move alongside, and then with a reassuring glance back to Blake and the others, he sat down beside her.

"I made the Hunter simulants to ensure no trace of humanity could ever return here," rasped Adra, her once powerful voice growing feebler by the second. "It pleased me to know that these simulants I created with human brains – beings who believed themselves to be human – would be responsible for humanity's end." She locked eyes with Taylor, and though her stare was glassy, it conveyed no less hatred, "Now look at what you've done."

As Taylor listened to Adra speak, unfiltered and unguarded for the first time, he found a part of himself empathize with her, and this shocked him more deeply than almost anything he had experienced since the revelation of his own identity. He'd hated the Hedalt for what they had done. Adra seemed not to see the irony that by creating human simulants, her race was no better than the Masters, who had engineered and used them. Yet despite what she had done, and despite the extreme measures the Hedalt had taken, Taylor understood the root cause of their resentment. What had happened to them was unjust. But it did not excuse what Warfare Command and Adra herself had done. They had sought to annihilate an entire species, and had come perilously close to succeeding, simply because humans had inherited a world that had been stolen from them. Despite human history, and the harm they had done to the planet over thousands of years, humans were not responsible for what happened to the Hedaltus. Of that crime, at least, they were blameless.

"You have no more claim to Earth than any of the creatures living on it, humans included," said Taylor, watching the sun dance off the slowly undulating water. "All I've done is help to right a wrong. What the humans do from here is down to them, and them alone. They can choose to be better than they were, or the same. They can cherish this re-birthed planet you have created, or turn it to ash. It was never for you to decide their fate."

Adra laughed again and more blood leaked out from the corner of her mouth. "Only fools believe in fate, simulant," she said, slowly twisting her neck to look at him. "And only the weak and unworthy are afraid to perform acts of greatness." Then she turned her head out to the water one last time, and added, with a melancholy that sounded almost human, "But I told you that you would not understand." Her eyelids flickered and the laser sharpness departed her eyes. Then she exhaled slowly, releasing her final breath into the warm evening air, and rested her head on the sand. "because despite everything... part of you is still... human..."

TWENTY-NINE

A crisp wind swept across the Colombia River, causing Sarah Sonner to pull her jacket more tightly around her body. Despite it being early Summer, the effect of wind-chill from the fresh river breeze was still bracing, and to cap it all off, it had just started to rain. She glanced at Taylor, who appeared not to be fazed by the temperature or the droplets of water landing on his smooth, synthetic skin. He was standing perfectly still, staring out towards Point Ellis, in the place where the Astoria-Megler Bridge used to be. Now the bridge, all signs of human habitation and everything in the city he had a memory of once calling home had been erased, and the area given back to nature. He didn't know which was more unreal – the memory of his former home or the sight of it now, as if he were looking at it through the lens of time.

"You know, I would have preferred that we had this little meeting back in California," complained Sonner, wiping the rain from her eyes. "I hate the rain."

"Add it to the list," said Taylor, smiling at her. "Besides coffee, is there anything you do actually like?"

This forced Sonner to think. For years leading up to the end of Earth's first war with the Hedalt, and all the time since she'd woken up, alone, in the Contingency base three centuries later, she'd thought of nothing but the fight. Now it was over, she didn't know what to think or how to feel.

"I guess I'm going to have to find a hobby or two."

"From what I've heard, Governor Sonner, you're not going to have time," Taylor said, teasing her by stressing the word 'Governor'.

Sonner just wafted a hand at him and tutted, "That's not a real title, it's just a..." she tried to come up with another description, but Taylor helped her out.

"It's a term of endearment. Affection even," said Taylor. "They all look up to you, as well they should. You've given them their home back."

Sonner shook her head, "Don't do that."

"Do what?"

"Write yourself out of the history books, before

the ink is even dry. Without you, none of this would have been possible. And this is your home too, remember?"

Taylor accepted her words without complaint, though he knew the time would soon come when he'd have to tell Sonner his plans. But right now, he was just enjoying her company, and the view.

"I'm sorry that Reese didn't get to see this," he said, reminded of others whose acts of heroism deserved recognition. "Whoever writes the history of The Contingency War should dedicate a chapter to him."

Sonner sighed, but then nodded slowly. "You know, he asked if I'd give it a second chance," she said, glancing back at Taylor. "He and I. It never even occurred to me that he wouldn't be here. You just assume the people you know will still be there at the end."

"I'm sorry," said Taylor, "I shouldn't have mentioned him. It was insensitive..."

"No, it's okay, really," Sonner interrupted, patting him gently on the shoulder, "I'm glad I at least got a chance to square things with him. But it's a shame he didn't get to see Earth again. He loved nature and the outdoors. He would have wanted to explore; to see everything." Then she laughed, "I was never really a believer in second chances..."

"Too stubborn, you mean..." said Taylor with a

smirk, and this time Sonner jabbed him on the arm.

"Fine, I was too stubborn to believe in second chances," Sonner corrected, "but after seeing what the Hedalt did to this planet, it just shows that anything is possible."

"You gave me a second chance," said Taylor, "As usual, you're too hard on yourself."

"I gave you a first chance, Taylor. You never needed a second." Then she looked at him with kind eyes and added, "Just another thing about you that's extremely rare."

Taylor smiled back and then peered out across the choppy water again, "I still can't get over the fact that the Hedalt were native to Earth."

"It doesn't excuse what they did," said Sonner, with an icy sharpness.

"Not all the Hedalt were like Adra," said Taylor, remembering Rikov and wondering how many millions, even billions more like him there were. "Warfare Command may never give up trying to claim Earth as their own, but there may still be other Hedalt on the planet, and they're not your enemy."

"I've actually given that some thought," said Sonner, as another gust of wind cut through the thin jacket she was wearing. "With the War Carrier, plus its fighters and a dozen other Hedalt cruisers we managed to salvage, added to the Nimrod Fleet, I'm not worried about Warfare

Command. But Adra's crimes, and the crimes of those like her shouldn't be shared by the innocent."

"So what do you intend to do about the Hedalt who are already on the planet?"

"They can stay," shrugged Sonner. "After all, if Adra is right, it's as much their world as ours. And it's hardly overpopulated right now."

Taylor smiled and shook his head, "Just when I thought I had you all figured out, you surprise the hell out of me again."

"I'm a complicated woman," Sonner replied, winking at him. "Just as this war was more complicated than we thought, too. We were naive to think the Hedalt were all the same. Evil, for want of a better word."

"It's easy to fight a war when you just see the enemy as monsters," said Taylor, remembering how Adra's programming had once made him see humans that way. Then he added, with a wink of his own, "A wise person told me that once."

The sky rumbled and Sonner looked up, squinting as heavier water droplets fell into her eyes, "Damn, I think there's a storm coming."

"It's not a storm," said Taylor, pointing up to an area of dark cloud. "It's just my ride."

Sonner traced the direction of Taylor's outstretched arm and saw the familiar, scorpion-like shape of a Hedalt Corvette soaring down from the upper atmosphere towards them.

"Which brings me to the thing I've been meaning to tell you," said Taylor, looking down and scuffing the soles of his boots in the dirt.

"You're not staying on Earth," said Sonner, without the slightest suggestion of surprise.

"No..." said Taylor, caught off guard. "You already knew?"

"I guessed," said Sonner, "I suppose I've had a nagging feeling for some time. It seemed like each time you found a new member of your crew, you were discovering a new part of yourself too. And that person became less and less the Taylor Ray that originated here, centuries ago."

"I can't really explain it better," said Taylor, again impressed by Sonner's sudden emotional insight. "It's as if I know this place, even without all the people, and the buildings and the bridge, but it's like remembering a photograph. I was never really here. This planet was never my home. And when you boil it down to the cold, hard facts, I'm not really human. I have no place here."

"I don't know what you are, my strange robotic friend," said Sonner, hooking her arm through Taylor's. "But your humanity is without question. And if you ever want to come back, Earth will always be your home."

The Contingency One circled round in front of them, its thrusters kicking up a trail of spray along the river adding yet more water into the already rain-saturated air. It then set down about twenty meters from where Sonner and Taylor were standing on the bank where the Maritime Memorial had once been. The rear cargo ramp lowered and soon Blake, Casey and Satomi all stepped out.

"I have one last favor to ask of you, Captain Taylor Ray," said Sonner as they walked together, arm in arm, towards the ship.

"Name it."

"I want you to destroy the super-luminal transceiver that's positioned near Earth," said Sonner, briefly adopting her more 'Commanderly' tone, "and any others that are close to the solar system. We need time to heal and re-build."

"Are you sure?" said Taylor, "Destroying them won't completely isolate Earth. They still know where you are."

"I know, but it will force them to have to make many blind jumps, which we know the Hedalt can't tolerate," said Sonner. "If nothing else, it will deter them from trying, and buy us more time."

"Aye aye, Commander Sarah Sonner," said Taylor as they both reached the ship and turned to face each other.

"Just Sarah will do fine," said Sonner.

Taylor was usually the awkward one in moments like these, but this time he knew exactly what to do. He reached out and pulled Sonner into a tight embrace, so tight that he actually heard joints in her spine clicking. But it didn't stop Sonner from reciprocating; squeezing back with just as much pressure. They remained this way for a couple more seconds, before they drew back and smiled warmly into each other's eyes.

"I'm going to miss you, Sarah," said Taylor.

"Likewise, Taylor," Sonner answered, "But I'm glad you got your family back. Take care out there, okay?"

"I will," said Taylor, "and thank you. For everything." Then he took a step towards his waiting crew, but paused and glanced back, "Well, everything apart from all the coffee cups you kept leaving around the ship."

Sonner laughed, as Taylor resumed his climb up the cargo ramp to join the others, who all waved at her, including, much to her surprise, the normally apathetic Blake Meade. The cargo ramp began to whir shut and Sonner backed away to get clear of the blast from the thrusters. She was wet enough already, without the engines blowing her into the chilly Columbia River. Then as the Contingency One gently lifted off and began to ascend, Sonner had the nagging feeling that she'd forgotten something, or left something unsaid. She wore a frown all the way back to the small Hedalt shuttlecraft they had commandeered to reach

Astoria in the first place, before it suddenly dawned on her.

She shot an uncharacteristically blue curse into the rainy Oregon sky and then called out after the rapidly vanishing shape of the Contingency One, "Damn it, Taylor, you still have my favorite mug!"

THIRTY

The crew of the Contingency One watched on the viewport as the super-luminal transceiver exploded brightly, burning like a miniature star, until eventually it fizzled into nothing, leaving only an expanding cloud of charred debris behind. With its destruction, another thread of the Fabric was also cut. Along with the other transceivers that they'd already destroyed, Taylor and his crew had torn a tiny hole in the vast, ancient network, wide enough to afford Earth a little breathing space from the Hedalt.

Still, Taylor knew that without destroying hundreds of transceivers it would still be possible for a ship to blind jump to Earth, calculating the course using other intersecting nodes. But Sonner was right that even this small tear would thwart the Hedalt's efforts to return. Without simulants, they would need to crew the ships themselves, and few Hedalt were as resilient to space travel as the indomitable Vice Provost Adra had been. But Taylor believed the precaution was still worth taking. Should Warfare Command survive the loss of the Nexus, there was always a possibility they would attempt to return and attack Earth again.

"That's the last of the spiky spaceballs, Cap," said Blake, flexing his arms as if he'd physically pummeled the transceiver into dust with his bare fists, rather than the ship's cannons.

"So, where to now, Cap?" asked Casey, spinning around in her chair, her sequined purple sneakers dancing in the air. Taylor smiled, suddenly realizing that they were similar to the pair that the original Casey Valera had worn. The new Casey must have found them in her quarters.

Taylor shrugged, "Anywhere we like," he said, nonplussed by the question. "We have enough fuel to fly twice around the galaxy if we want to, so I'll leave it up to you. Pilot's discretion!"

Blake shuddered, "I ain't sure that 'pilot's discretion' is such a great idea when it comes to Casey," he said, tilting his head back to look at Taylor, "She'll end up flyin' us through a nebula or into a black hole, just for kicks."

"Ooh, a black hole sounds like *fun*..." Casey answered, pressing a finger to her bottom lip, as if she were a super-villain contemplating a new master plan. "But, as luck would have it, I've computed a few interesting destinations, already." Then she winked at Blake, "One is even close to a black hole..." she added, before turning back to Taylor. "So, give the word, Cap, and let's explore!"

Taylor thought for a moment and then smiled, "Second star to the right, and straight on till morning..." he annunciated.

Blake clicked his fingers repeatedly "Oh, wait, I know that one!" he called out with enthusiasm, and then he squeezed his eyes shut, "Damn it, I know it! It'll come to me... just wait... wait... Peter Pan! Right?" He looked at Taylor expectantly, and he nodded, clearly impressed. "I have a memory of my ma' – or Blake's ma, whatever – readin' it to me. I even know the author, J M Barrie." Then he stabbed an outstretched finger towards Satomi Rose, who had walked over beside Taylor and rested a hand on his shoulder. "There, how d'ya like that, Satomi? I actually got one of the Cap's quotes right!"

Satomi scrunched up her nose a little, "Well, almost right..." Taylor and Casey looked at her, expectantly, while Blake's face fell. "The true quote is, 'Second to the right, and straight on till morning.' The mention of a star was added to the later animated movie adaptations. So, technically speaking..."

"Oh no," Blake interrupted, wagging a finger at her, "don't you dare!"

"...technically speaking," Satomi continued, wearing an especially wicked smirk, "you are incorrect, Blake. Sorry."

Casey and Taylor burst out laughing, but Satomi managed to hold it together, despite her smile growing broader.

"Damn it, Cap, this Satomi's the worst of the lot!" said Blake, though he was smiling too. "Must be cos' she's a glitchy prototype."

"We're all prototypes, Blake," said Taylor, "the first and only of our kind. And I think it's about time we got underway." Then he turned back to Casey with a twinkle in his silver simulant eyes, and said, "Second star to the right, Casey."

"Aye aye, Captain Taylor Ray!" sang Casey, as she spun back around and selected one of her new jump programs at random; one which would take them into an unexplored region of the galaxy. She started the jump countdown and began to spin around in her chair, toes pointed and sequined sneakers sparkling like fire, "Hold on to your hats, people...

Jumping in five...

...F o u r

...T h r e e

. . . T   w   o

. . . O   n   e"

THIRTY-ONE

Personal Journal – Entry #4
   When I started this journal, I didn't know who I was. I'm still learning. But what I do know is that I'm not the same Taylor Ray that the Hedalt harvested over three hundred years ago. That Taylor was human. He lived on Earth in Astoria, Oregon, and called that place his home. And while a part of me may be human, Earth is not my home. My home is the Contingency One. And humans are not my family. Well, with one notable, and often cranky, caffeine-addicted, but ultimately exceptional exception. My family is right here with me – and my place is with them, out among the stars.

   We started together as a group of simulants living a cruel and devious lie, but though we were torn apart, we found each other again. None of us are the same people we thought we were, and each of us is still discovering what it truly means to be an individual. But we're doing it together. Somehow, we all share a bond that no other living creature in the galaxy has. We're linked through memories, new and old, real and imagined, and through a unique connection that's woven through the fabric of space itself. Each of us is special. Each of us is flawed. In that way, I guess we're not all that different to humans, after all.

I had no idea at the start of this journey where I'd end up. I'd made it my mission to find Casey Valera, Blake Meade and Satomi Rose again. Find them and lift the veil of lies so that they could see the universe as I saw it, free and alive. I don't know how we managed it, but we pulled it off. So now a new mission begins. A new journey. Where will it take us? I have no idea, but I'm excited to find out.

I also said I wanted Satomi to see what I saw and for us to gaze upon the galaxy of stars together with newborn eyes. But the truth is, she's already seen and shown me so much more. We were always together in our minds, joined through space and time, long before our physical forms ever met. Whenever times were darkest, we found each other. We saved each other. We're a part of one another. If that's not love, I don't know what is.

So, who am I? My name is Captain Taylor Ray, and I am awake.

The end.

THANK YOU

You made it! Thank you so much for reading The Contingency War series. I sincerely hope you enjoyed reading it as much as I enjoyed writing it.

If you did then perhaps consider leaving a review on Amazon, and also reading my post-apocalyptic military sci-fi series, The Planetsider Trilogy (details on the next page).

To stay up-to-date on future novels in this series, and other books by G J Ogden, please subscribe to the newsletter, which also includes great offers and free books from other indie SFF authors.

Thanks again – see you next time!

Best Wishes

http://subscribe.ogdenmedia.net/

ALSO BY THIS AUTHOR

If you enjoyed this book, please consider reading The Planetsider Trilogy, also by G J Ogden, available from Amazon.

The Planetsider Trilogy:
A post-apocalyptic thriller with a military Sci-Fi twist

- The Planetsider
- The Second Fall
- The Last of the Firsts

"The strong action sequences and thoughtful worldbuilding make this one worth picking up for fans of plot-driven SF." - **Publishers Weekly**

ABOUT THE AUTHOR

At school I was asked to write down the jobs I wanted to do as a 'grown up'. Number one was astronaut and number two was a PC games journalist. I only managed to achieve one of those goals (I'll let you guess which), but these two very different career options still neatly sum up my lifelong interests in science, space and the unknown.

School also steered me in the direction of a science-focused education over literature and writing, which influenced my decision to study physics at Manchester University. What this degree taught me is that I didn't like studying physics and instead enjoyed writing, which is why you're reading this book! The lesson? School can't tell you who you are.

When not writing, I enjoy spending time with my family, walking in the British countryside, and indulging in as much Sci-Fi as possible.

You can connect with me here:
https://twitter.com/GJ_Ogden
https://www.facebook.com/PlanetsiderNovel

Subscribe to my newsletter:
http://subscribe.ogdenmedia.net

Made in the USA
Monee, IL
26 February 2022

91889942R10173